LUCY SCOTT'S GRAND STAND

Also by Alan Sorem

Time

LUCY SCOTT'S GRAND STAND

Age Is an Attitude, Not a Condition

A Novel

Alan Sorem

RESOURCE *Publications* · Eugene, Oregon

LUCY SCOTT'S GRAND STAND
Age Is an Attitude, Not a Condition

Resource Publications
An Imprint of Wipf and Stock Publishers
199 W. 8th Ave., Suite 3
Eugene, OR 97401

www.wipfandstock.com

ISBN 13: 978-1-4982-0107-0

Manufactured in the U.S.A.   07/23/2014

Some of the text in this novel first appeared in the musical
Lucy Scott's Grand Stand, copyright © 2013 Alan Sorem.

For Elizabeth and John

Fides et Fortis

Preface

My name is Lucy Royster Scott. This is my book. I've written it to give other older people courage to take a stand for the life they want rather than what the world dictates.

At times it takes a while for me to remember a name, an address, or a date. I've heard that the brain is a magnificent computer that in our later years is so full of data that it may require extra time for sorting information requested. I sometimes take naps in the afternoon. I usually go to bed no later than nine o'clock and rise by six.

I am not feeble, infirm or disengaged from life. Respect my opinion: Age is an attitude, not a condition.

I have always lived in Brooklyn, New York. I grew up in Bay Ridge an only child, rare in my neighborhood. My parents shipped me off to my maternal grandmother in Sparta, New Jersey during the summers.

My grandmother was born in 1876. She was a widow and enormously proud of her deceased husband, a West Point graduate who died in France in 1917. Her views on manners were very precise and my activities prompted her to say often during my summer visits, "Lucy, so unladylike!"

She disliked it when I rolled down the grassy hill in her backyard, when I stuck my tongue out at older boys when they sauntered by on the sidewalk, or put my chewing gum under the front pew at church on Sundays, and especially when I whistled a John Philip Sousa march while washing dishes after supper.

Nevertheless I adored her. She had backbone. She could sniff at my antics, but if anyone else expressed an opinion about my behavior, they received an icy stare from her cold blue eyes.

I think it was her stories about her husband and the letters she read to me from wartime France that prompted my early curiosity about all things French.

I live in The Russell House, a comfortable Brooklyn apartment house built in 1926 by Roy Russell across from the Park. It was his first major construction project and he designed it with high ceilings and spacious rooms with grand views because he and his family were to live there.

October 24th, 2013 was my 85th birthday, the sixty-first birthday I have celebrated since my husband and I moved into The Russell House. Jim is gone now, and of the three bedrooms, two are storage rooms of memorabilia for his awards at the Brooklyn Navy Yard and items from the lives of my three children.

But enough of all that. On the eve of my birthday, I had a fairly usual Wednesday: Aqua-aerobics at eleven in the pool at the community center, then a light lunch at the café nearby. I returned books to the Public Library and checked out a romantic novel by one of my favorite authors. I went on to the high school to meet with three students for French tutoring. Afterwards I picked up my special treat at The Bagel Hole on 7th Avenue and made my way home to enjoy two halves of a lovely poppy seed bagel with cream cheese, lox, Bermuda onion and sliced tomato.

After my feast I passed on the evening news and settled in for my annual pre-birthday reading of selected items in my packet of letters I have saved over the years. I always begin with two letters from my mother's brother, dear Uncle Paul. And this year I will end with a letter that Mr. K slipped under my door recently.

1

Dear Whistler,

Thank you for your letter. Straight A's! Your good grades are an example to all of us working in the war effort here on the West Coast.

I apologize for missing your birthday. Please forgive me. I was busy becoming a married man.

The lucky woman is Constance Sawyer (goes by "Connie"), who is a very accomplished pianist for the junior high Sunday School and teaches math in high school. You will meet her whenever we can make the trip back East.

I agree that the news from Guadalcanal is bad, and, along with you I am very sorry for the parents of the five Sullivan brothers who went down with the USS Juneau. I recommend five whistles of *Stars and Stripes Forever* to honor their sons.

We must keep our spirits up and support our fighting men. Rommel is on the run in North Africa. The Nazi attempt to take Stalingrad has failed. They should have learned from Napoleon!

Give my regards to your parents. If your mother seems overly strict at times, please remember she loves you and wants the best for you, as does your father. If that doesn't work, remind her about the time Stinky Smith hit her in the face with a snowball and I beat the tar out of him. That should make her smile!

Affectionately,
Uncle Paul

Seattle, Washington
June 8, 1944

Dear Favorite Niece (yes, you are my only niece but you still are my favorite),

Thank you for your letter. You certainly are mopping up the opposition with your academic record! And in answer to your question, my work is going well at the factory.

Our boys and the Allies are doing a great job. What an enormous effort D-Day was, and I am glad it paid off! And Rome has fallen so the rest of Italy should be easy. Mr. Mussolini will be running scared. I hope for good news from the Pacific.

Our son Paul Junior is doing fine and I am busting my buttons as the proud father! At the rate he is crawling (here he is at my chair as I write), I figure he will be walking soon.

Have a good summer working at the Y Camp. Teach those young hooligans nasty words in French. They'll eat it up.

Give my regards to your parents. If they seem strict about not dating until you graduate, just remember that from their point of view they are fearful it will lead to kissing and (*quelle horreur!*) canoodling! Notice how I worked a French phrase in to make you smile.

Affectionately,
Uncle Paul

Milo Oberson High School
212 Park Place
Brooklyn, N.Y.

June 12, 1946

Dear Miss Royster:

I am writing to commend you for your excellent academic record in your high school years. I join with your parents in their pride for your achievements.

I understand that you will continue with your study of the French language to prepare for a position as translator at the new United Nations edifice in Manhattan. My very best wishes to you in all your endeavors. I am sure you will do well.

Sincerely,

M. Edgar Jones
Principal

Sparta, N.Y.
June 20, 1946

Dear Lucile,

I am so very proud of you. Your mother sent me a copy of your vale-
dictory address at the high school commencement exercises. A very
good speech except for the whistling at the conclusion.

Ah, well. If you are going to be a hellion, at least you will be a well-
educated one. I am being humorous.

Sincerely,
Your Grandmother
Mrs. Zachary P. Thomas

Millvale and Duboise
321 Madison Avenue
New York, NY

August 23, 1946

Miss Lucile Royster:

With this letter I confirm your employment with Millvale and Duboise as a General Management Aide, commencing Tuesday, September 3 at 8:00 a.m. At that time, please report to my office for your introduction to other staff and your desk assignment. Your remuneration will be $72.00 per week, less deductions, with seven (7) paid holidays and one week paid vacation annually.

All of us at Millvale and Duboise look forward to your employment with us.

Sincerely yours,

G. Philip Duboise, Jr.
Personnel Officer
GPD, Jr./avc

The Bronx, N.Y.
December 5, 1950

My dear Lucy,

Please forgive me for telephoning you at the office yesterday afternoon about Roy. The Army Officers rang my doorbell at 1:30 pm to give me the news that my son was killed in action at Chosin Reservoir on the 30th, as was most of B Company, 31st Infantry. I was so agitated that they called my next-door neighbor in to sit with me. That is when I telephoned you. I simply did not know what else to do except to share our grief together.

Roy loved you very much and was looking forward to the wedding once he had fulfilled his military duty.

Please come and see me when you can.

Warmly,
Mrs. Roy Puller, Sr.

My dear child,

You mother called to tell me of Roy's death in Korea. I join you in your grief.

Always remember that Roy died a hero for his country against the godless Chinese and Koreans.

It is Pearl Harbor Day as I write you. The defense of freedom carries a high price, as my husband often said. He, too, paid the price. Now, regrettably, you and I have a stronger common bond through the men we loved.

Your mother says you have been given a week off. Please come and see me and we shall console each other.

With deepest sympathy,
Your Grandmother
Mrs. Zachary P. Thomas

Dear Lucile:

After your mother informed me of your elopement, I pressured her to tell me of your new address and at last she has sent it to me.

I will speak to you plainly. You are old enough to have a handle on life, and if your heart has led you to James Scott I say, God bless your union. Now for something even your mother does not know. When I was your age, I ran off with a dashing Army lieutenant named Zachary Paul Thomas, much against my parents' wishes and warnings. My mother was a martinet, and I regret to say I am more like her than I wish to admit. However, Zach and I had a wonderful marriage and three wonderful children. May you be so blessed as well.

Life as an Army wife was not easy. Your life with James will not be easy. But if you are true to each other and able to overcome difficulties together, you will have the joy of shared memories later on.

I have appreciated our conversations and confidences in recent years. Please come and see me – with James – when it is possible for you to do so.

And do remember: your parents' hurt and feelings of rejection will heal. You are their only child and they will not want to lose you forever. We all have the ability, if we choose to use it, to come to terms with uncomfortable facts. My parents did and so will yours.

Your Loving Grandmother,
Mrs. Zachary P. Thomas

May 24, 1953

Dear Precious Lucy,

We have a first anniversary celebration dinner with our friends at Stragoni's on the day you will receive this, but you know how tongue-tied I get when sentiment is involved. So I am putting my thoughts on paper.

You are a wonderful wife and I am honored to be your husband. A year ago it was all such a whirl. We survived! We both know that first month wasn't easy. Thanks to our mutual love and sense of humor (did I really say "waffle leaded wife" in my vows?), the rest of the year has been great.

I am so glad you enjoy being on top. I love to hear your laughter!

Jim

Tampa, Florida
October 17, 1976

Dear Lucy,

Thank you for taking time away from your husband and the school to come for your father's funeral. I would have figured out the checking account and other financial matters by myself but I appreciated your help.

It was good to see the photos of your children. My goodness, they're all grown up now. And I do wish you would consider spending more time in the Florida sunshine. How you can stand winters in New York is beyond me.

Mom

November 28, 2003

Hi, Mom.

It was great to have another Skype face-to-face the day before Thanks-giving. I saw Abe Weinstein hovering behind you. Please thank him again from me for letting you use his computer for our connection. And give my thanks to the church ladies for sending along a lovely package!

There was a big surprise for our Thanksgiving meal here. Because of the censors I cannot tell you who came. A very high official and a good time was had by all. It was real lift to our spirits!

Going with a convoy tomorrow. Wish me safe travel.

Give a big hello from me to Brother Jim and Sister Sophie. I will send you some more Iraqi jokes to pass on to them.

Will try for another Skype session after I return. I'll let Abe know by the usual channels.

Love you,
Steve

Rev. Dr. Roger Willoughby
Asbury Court United Methodist Church
Brooklyn, New York 11215

December 5, 2003

Dear Mrs. Scott,

Thank you for the opportunity to have prayer together yesterday. I join you in your grief at the loss of your son, Lt. Colonel Steve Scott.

As I promised, I did speak to the local Army people here in Brooklyn and they confirm that his body should be released from Dover Air Base early next week. By then you will need to have told me whether or not you wish to have a funeral service here first or just a simple committal service at Arlington Cemetery. If you wish to use the church, the ladies of the Abigail Circle will be glad to hold a reception afterwards in the Church Parlor.

Please give my warmest regards to your son and daughter. I look forward to meeting them here or in Washington. Christ's love comforts us all in this time of sorrow.

Sincerely,
Pastor Roger

128 Stoll Avenue
Louisville, KY 40206
July 22, 2013

Dear GGM* Lucy,

You are really great! Thank you again for helping me with the video for my communications class this summer at U of L. Everybody I know has seen it and they all are impressed with your vitality as your 85th birthday approaches. In the last three weeks *Age Is an Attitude, Not a Condition* has scored 10,500 hits on the internet. Wow! Not bad for a first try, huh?

I did not see Granddad Jim and his wife while I was in NYC that weekend. He was busy at some conference or something. As you know, my father and Granddad Jim had a falling out some years ago. Over what, I've never discovered but I suspect it was about Granddad's divorce from Dad's mom Kate. I should have asked you when I had the chance, but it really is ancient history for me. I like to think about the future and not the past.

Please thank Fred for letting me stay at his apartment for the weekend. You and Fred are "the real thing!"

Above is my new address. It is a three-room (plus kitchen and bath) "shotgun house." That is the description for old houses in this part of the 'Ville. All the doors are in line, so if you open the front door, it is said you could fire a shotgun all the way through! My friend Ray and I are sharing the space. (No shotguns allowed!)

The other excitement here is the football and basketball teams, as well as baseball and women's basketball teams, who all look good to repeat their successes of last year. Go, Cards!

Affectionately, your GGS,
Alex

*I am using GGM because it is easier than Great Grandmother.

September 9, 2013

Mon très estimé professeur,

Merci beaucoup pour notre conversation d'aujourd'hui. Elle a réveillé beaucoup de bons et tendres souvenirs de ma mère et des conversations que nous avons partagées, du professeur de français qui vous a suivi à Johnson Tech, des gens que j'aide (la plupart des haïtiens) quand ils viennent à la pharmacie pour les ordonnances. Mais maintenant je passé à l'anglais. Je peux bavarder en français, "la belle langue," mais je trouve que c'est plus difficile de écrire en français.

[For those readers not conversant in French, I have translated Mr. K's first paragraph. *"Esteemed Professor: Thank you very much for our conversation today. It brought back many warm memories — of my mother and the conversations we would have, of the French teacher who followed you at Johnson Tech, of the people whom I help (mostly Haitian) when they come for prescriptions at the pharmacy. But now I switch to English. I can chatter away in 'the beautiful language', but I find it more difficult when it comes to the written word."*]

I find it very pleasant to converse with you. I am glad to hear that your successor, Madam Bonner, is still holding forth at school. She frequently expressed her chagrin when I would mix up my tenses. During our last conversation in the lobby, please forgive my silence when you asked me what my name is. I told you my surname is Dugay. I did not know how to respond when you then asked what Mr. K stands for. Please forgive me if I seemed rude as I turned away.

Let me tell you now, but I beg your patience as I recite some family history.

My mother, Lucinda Dugay, was born in French Guiana in South America. The family had moderate means to support her older sister and her two younger brothers. When my mother was eighteen, she became involved with a man of low repute and her parents sent her to live with her older sister, Violet, who by then was working in a pharmacy in Manhattan while she pursued a pharmacy degree. Violet agreed to let my mother stay with her rent-free on the condition that she also enroll in a pharmacy program. She did so.

By age twenty-five she had her pharmacy degree and was employed at a pharmacy in Brooklyn. Shortly after she began there, one of her customers took a liking to her and asked her out. They hit it off. She moved out of Violet's apartment and into his. He was a rising Big Name in racial matters in Manhattan.

Her father, alerted by Violet, came to New York to dissuade her from the relationship. She would not, she told him, because she was pregnant by the man and he had promised to marry her.

I was born on December 26, 1987. He gave me my name, Kwanzaa, the African-American celebration that begins on the 26th. My father by then supervised the local office of a congressman from New York City. Two weeks after my birth he was promoted to a staff position in Washington and left my mother with no marriage and no support. He claimed that she had had affairs with other men, one of whom was the actual father. She countered his claim, stating that he was the only man in her life.

Unfortunately there was no such thing as DNA testing in those days. Nevertheless, an understanding administrator ruled that she was eligible for child support. My father protested but, to avoid controversy harmful to his career, he paid up.

I have attempted several times to be in touch with my father. My letters were never answered. On a high school tour to Washington, I went to the congressman's office where he was employed. The receptionist told me he was not available. When I said I was his son and would wait, she gave me a hard look and repeated that he was not available.

I wish to retain a tie to the man who fathered me. But I will not use the name he gave me.

That is why I go by "Mr. K."

My mother subsequently never married. She returned to her work in the pharmacy, found day care for me, and insisted from my youngest years that I would follow in her steps.

In high school I took French because she wanted me to learn "better French" than the conversations we had in her Guianese version.

In many ways I was a disappointment to my mother. My grades were okay but not as outstanding as she had hoped. In my college years I was involved in a rap group as lead singer. That pretty much led nowhere, though we still do occasional gigs in the older establishments in DUMBO. (That may be an unknown term to you: Downtown Under the Manhattan Bridge Overpass.) My mother pressured me to follow the family path toward a professional pharmacy degree, and she knew the right people to make it happen for me. She also found a job for me as an assistant at the CVS pharmacy where you have your prescriptions.

My mother died of breast cancer two years ago. I took care of her until the end. When she died, one of her brothers insisted that she be buried in the family plot. I accompanied the coffin to her hometown, Cayenne. It was my first visit. I found the people friendly, especially my Uncle Christophe, who received a doctorate from MIT and is involved back home as senior staff at ESA, the European Space Agency. You may have heard of their Ariane launches. ESA is a commercial rival to American launches, though I hear NASA and others are considering the same kind of thing.

My uncle wanted me to stay on, but I am too American to want to live somewhere else.

I continue to wish to be known as Mr. K, and I know you will respect this.

Several months ago, I tired of living in my mother's apartment. Too many memories. Also, I wished to find a place nearer my work and also near subway connections to my degree program.

During my search, Carlos Morales came in the drug store one day. He was a classmate of mine at Tech. I recognized him and we fell into a conversation. He knew of a one-bedroom vacancy here at The Russell House, and here I am.

On another subject, please know that I very much would like to be involved in the weekend supplemental food program for needy students at the elementary school nearby. I think you said Thursday evenings are when the group meets in your apartment to do this.

Encore, mes remerciements, [Again, my thanks.]

Mr. K

2

As a rule I sleep in on my birthdays and my 85th was no exception. It was a bit of pampering Big Jim always had insisted on.

I had a muffin and a cup of decaf in bed and enjoyed a lovely long soak in the tub with extra bubble bath and aromatic candles. I was just finishing with my makeup when I heard the murmur of a man's voice through the closed door in the hallway that leads to the kitchen.

The voice rose and fell. I recognized it as Jim Junior's voice. Odd. He has a key, but he usually called before dropping by.

Throwing on my bathrobe, I walked out of the bedroom and listened intently behind the door to the kitchen. He was speaking to someone, but the only voice I heard was his. It was his Angry Voice. I call him Mr. Boom-Boom when he uses it on me.

Quietly I opened the door.

My son stood by the kitchen table, his back to me, speaking on his cell phone. I realized he was speaking to his sister Sophie. He had pushed aside the dozen or so birthday cards that were propped up on the table to make room for his briefcase. As he spoke, his free hand periodically drummed on the top of the fine leather briefcase that lay on the table. He obviously was irritated.

"Sis, I'm over at her place now. Stopped by after the mayor's Business Council meeting to wish Mom a Happy Birthday. Looks like she hasn't washed her dishes for a couple of days. We've got to do something. Mom needs help. She can't live alone." He paused.

"I *know* you have involvements!"

An audible sputter from the other side.

"I don't care who you sleep with; it's Mom who's home alone. It's clear we've got to do something. You have your life; I have mine. I can't spend mine running over to Brooklyn to make sure she's okay. Winter is coming and Mom's not safe alone."

A longer pause. I could hear irritation in Sophie's voice but I could not make out the words.

"You're living *together* now and your partner's name is Pru? And her daughter also will be living with you! What about the woman who calls *you* her daughter? You ought to visit more often, Sis. She's going downhill. Each time I visit her she's taking more pills. I'm gonna guess her best days are through."

I entered the conversation. *"Je vais très bien, merci beaucoup!"*

He turned his angry face my way and waved me silent.

"The French teacher just got up. Look, I've got to go."

More sputtering on the other end.

"Sis, you're the counselor, the one who has the tact. And you're the one to do this. All those fancy degrees! Make 'em useful!"

An explosion of anger on the other end of the phone. He responded in kind.

"No, no. Don't make it my duty! My duty was Dad! I know it was fifteen years ago but I remember it like it was yesterday. Don't you remember? You were tied up with — Oh, oh, she's watching me now. Are her hearing aids in? She's going to *parlez vous* in French again!"

I was totally exasperated. *"Je ne suis pas sourde! Je peux entendre!"*

My son turned away.

I walked over to the kitchen sink. I needed something physical to do, so I began to wash the dishes and put them in the drying rack.

All I could think about was how it used to be when he was a youngster. Our first child. The Saturdays when Jim and I and Little Jim played in the park.

Now all he ever thinks about are fortune and fame. Money, always more money. Mr. Big Corporate Executive. The charity balls and the pictures of him and his third wife on the society pages. He commutes to Manhattan from Chappaqua and buys her a new Cadillac every Christmas. Dear God, whatever happened to simple living?

They're very intense people, Jim Junior and his sister. But the middle one, Steve, he was like his father. He had the same hearty laugh. When problems arose his favorite saying was, "This too shall pass."

If he had lived, I know he'd say these other two are daft.

My son's voice escalated as he began pacing to the kitchen service door and back.

"Sophie, you're involved in all of this with me. C'mon, Sis, how stupid can you be! *WE* have got to do something. Winter is coming and Mom can't live alone!"

An angry voice erupted on the other end. He cut in.

"Well, getting totally pissed off does not get us anywhere. Just listen to me, will you?

"Here is the situation. Her days are all a tangle. She takes morning pills at night!"

He paused.

"Yes, yes, I know you got her the seven-day pill box with blue on one side for morning and red on the other for night, but she *still gets them messed up!* And I'm looking at her right now. One in the afternoon and she's in her bathrobe. Not the one you gave her, either, it's the old ratty one."

He paused. I finished up the dishes and turned to face him.

He looked directly at me as he spoke into the phone. "Well, looks like I'm in the doghouse now. Time to do it."

He held the cell phone away from his ear. He spoke loudly.

"Mom, can you hear me?"

I nodded. "Yes, I can hear every word."

He lowered his voice. "Mom, Sis and I know what's best for you. A quiet place where you won't have to worry about a thing. Help with keeping your pills straight. Good meals, good nursing care—in a place that you can afford."

"But this has been my home—our home—for more than fifty years. My daughter and my son! Why are you plotting against me?"

He turned away again, his voice triumphant.

"There, Sis, did you hear? A touch of paranoia, right? She's losing her marbles; it's worse than last year! Yes, now we've got to do something. Winter is coming and Mom can't live alone."

How could I make him and his sister listen? They had it all wrong.

"Yes, winter is coming but I am *not* alone! I have good friends and neighbors here! Why put me away in some strange place? Can you hear *me*?"

"You have to face the facts, Mom. Even your doctor says so!"

"You talked to *my doctor*!"

"He told me about the time you left your purse on the receptionist's desk and she had to run all the way to the bus stop after you. He says your blood pressure is way, way too high. Yet you refuse to do anything about it."

"My doctor told you this? Whatever happened to patient confidentiality!"

"Mom, I'm just getting started. He also said—"

"It doesn't matter! I'm *always* tense when I go see him. Ever since I finally persuaded your father to go, and then came the bombshell about his cancer—"

"Mom, be reasonable!"

"I *am* reasonable. I just have a severe case of, what do they call it? White-coat syndrome. I walk through that office door, every part of me tenses up."

"Listen to me, Mom. I need to go pay some attention to the company's clients in London. Leaving tomorrow. Two weeks. Betsy is going too, for shopping and shows. So I won't be around, and Sis is tied up. We need to find an affordable place for you where professionals will take care of you. Face it. It's time."

"You—you feel like you're responsible for me. But you're not! I'm responsible for me! If I need help, I have plenty of friends here!"

He smiled, ignored my protests, and turned his back to me once again.

"Sis, thanks so much. I'm glad we can agree. Gotta go, now. I'll be in touch. Ciao."

The cell phone went back into his shirt pocket.

"Don't worry, Mom. Sis and I will get it all worked out."

"You don't need to get it all worked out," I hissed.

"Well, who else, Mom? Who else?"

He looked around. "Everything has been the same since Dad died. Time for a change."

As he lifted his slim designer briefcase from the table, several of my birthday cards fell to the floor. He leaned, picked them up and placed them on the table before moving toward the door.

"Gotta go, Mom. Got a big deal cooking. You take care, Mom."

"You've always got a big deal cooking."

He turned. "Mom, don't start in on me. I'm not in the mood for it today."

"I'm happy where I am."

"Sure. For how long? Answer me that. For how long?"

"I want to die here."

"That's just great. Let me tell you something."

We were spitting words back and forth.

"I am about to be named the president and CEO of my company. That's what I've wanted for a long time. I also want to get you into a place that will take good care of you." His voice rose. "I don't have the time for it any more."

"You've never had the time. It's all about you. You're just a never-satisfied striver."

He put his briefcase back on the table. He gave me a long look and laughed.

"That's good, Mom. That's really good. Who the hell do you think I got it from? Good ol' easy-going Dad? No. I got it from the person who was always best in class and wanted more. Wanted to go to college and did it. Wanted to be a French teacher and did it. You."

We glared at each other. He picked up the briefcase again.

"I am *your* product, Mom! Not easy-going Steve, your favorite. Not Sophie, always tied in knots trying to live up to your expectations. A thousand times you told me I could do better. I'm the one who's like you and I'm proud of it, even if you never understand. And I *am* going to the top, all the way, Mom, so get used to it and do as I say!"

"Never!"

"You stubborn woman!" He was shouting now. "You're going to get sick and die, just like Dad, and I don't want any part of it!"

"You listen to me!" I shouted back.

"I've spent a lifetime listening – now you listen to me!"

Five knocks on the door, ratta-tat-tat-tat.

He smoothed his hair back with his free hand. He took a deep breath and gave me a frown.

"Hope it's not those Pakistanis down the hall. Just another reason to move, Mom. The roaches swarm here from their place."

"Don't be ridiculous. She's a doctor. He has his Ph.D."

He didn't hear me as he turned away again.

"That's just fine, Mom. Gotta go. Driver's waiting. Remember, take your pills at the right time. Maybe they'll help. Bye, now."

He opened the door. "Oh, it's you."

My friend Daisy entered, a bottle of wine under her arm and carrying a saucer with a cupcake, a lighted candle in the middle of it.

Jim Junior turned back to me. "Two weeks, Mom."

As she entered, Daisy looked him up and down and said in a sarcastic tone, "Goodbye, Prince Charming."

My son rushed out and slammed the door as he left. Daisy shielded the candle from the breeze.

3

"WELL!" EXCLAIMED DAISY as my son slammed the door behind him. She took the cupcake and wine to the table. "Loud voices in here."

"We were arguing about my future."

"Well, I hope you won." She held up the bottle.

"Beaujolais for you, *mon ami*! How many is it, now?"

"Eighty-five."

"A lot of living, hon. Think of all we've been through in our lifetimes!"

Another knock at the door. Daisy was on her way to the kitchen to hunt for a corkscrew. I went to answer. It was my neighbor who lives up on six, Carlos Morales.

"Why, Carlos, what a pleasant surprise! Come in."

"Hi, Miss Lucy. It's teacher conference day at the elementary school, so Benjy and I wanted to come say Happy Birthday. Benjy has something he made this morning especially for you."

His seven-year-old son hung back, but Carlos urged him forward.

"This is for you," Benjy murmured. "Thank you for all your help."

He handed me a piece of paper folded in half. I opened it.

"Benjy, what a lovely card. Thank you."

He gave me a big smile and looked around. "Is there cake?"

"Not a big one. Daisy just brought me a cupcake and I'm sure she will be glad to give you half."

Daisy sliced half the cupcake and found a small plate.

"How's the job search going?" she asked Carlos as she brought the plate over to Benjy.

He grimaced and replied in a low tone so Benjy wouldn't hear.

"I had my fifteenth interview yesterday. With the consolidation going on, there's not a lot of demand for mid-level managers like me. But you know what they say, 'Hope springs eternal.'"

"You're certainly due. Rosa still has a job?"

"Yes, thank the good Lord and Bloomingdale's. And I still have some severance pay left."

Benjy had wolfed down his share of the cupcake. He eyed the other half on the table. His father smiled.

"Benjy and I are on our way to the playground."

I gave Benjy a big smile and hugged him.

"Benjy, it's a good, sunny day for the park. Thank you again for such a fine birthday card. I'm going to hang it on my wall next to my family picture."

4

DAISY AND I HAD just settled in for a long chat over our Beaujolais when there was a "shave and a haircut" knock at the service door.

"That's Abe Weinstein," I said. "He called last evening to ask if he could bring Rebecca down about now."

"He still seeing that widow in 1 C?"

I sighed and rose. "Daisy, I don't know. It's his business. I think he needs a break from Rebecca. You know how she's in and out of lucidity."

"I've seen Miz 1 C greet him at her door while I'm waiting for the elevator. Every hair in place, with a black dress on. She's so *glad* to see him."

"Shhh! Get another glass for Rebecca." I opened the door. "Hello. Rebecca."

I stood aside as Abe pushed the wheelchair in. Rebecca was nicely dressed but her hair lacked attention.

"Thank you, Lucy. Hi, Mrs. Van Horn."

Daisy gave a noncommittal grunt as she brought a third glass to the table and poured wine into it.

Abe pushed Rebecca's wheelchair to the table and looked down at her. "She's in a sad mood today," he said softly.

I smiled. "We'll cheer her up. We're having a party!"

"Just be a bit. An hour or so."

Daisy snorted and called after him as he left. "Don't do anything I wouldn't do!" But he was already out the door.

She and I lifted our glasses. Rebecca stared at hers as if it were an unknown object. Daisy and I exchanged looks.

I said, "Rebecca, it's wine. We're having a party."

"A party?"

"Yes, Rebecca." Daisy gave Rebecca a smile and gestured at her glass. "Today is Lucy's birthday. We're toasting her."

Rebecca returned the smile. "Your birthday?"

"No." A gesture at me. "Lucy's. Here's to Lucy!"

Rebecca stared at me and then lifted her glass. "To Lucy."

We drank ours down. Rebecca sipped slowly. At last she lowered her glass to the table and cried out, "*L'chaim!*"

"Ready for more?" Daisy asked.

"No thank you. It makes me tipsy and that's not a good thing."

"It's a special day." Daisy overrode her. She split the rest of the bottle between our glasses. The three of us sipped.

"Pretty quiet for a birthday," she said.

"I'm still thinking of what my son said."

"Oh."

"I can take care of myself just fine. And even when I can't, there's all kinds of home care."

Daisy nodded and lifted her glass.

"Here's to better times."

She and I drank and put our empty glasses down.

"Good wine," I noted. "Thank you."

Daisy eyed the empty bottle.

"I'll have to go up home and get some more."

"No, no, there's a half-bottle of Merlot in the 'frig."

"I have a song now," declared Rebecca.

"Here we go again," muttered Daisy. "C'mon, help me find the other bottle."

We rose and moved to the 'frig as Rebecca started to sing to herself in a low voice. She had a lovely alto voice. She had been a vocal music teacher for many years at a high school in Manhattan. A very good one, from what I've heard. A number of her students moved on to Broadway and opera. It's strange how the brain works. One part produces lovely songs even when the rest goes gaga.

Rebecca sang: "The clock ticks on, my circle's growing thin. I'm not at all sure who I am or where I've been."

"Very nice," I called out from the kitchen.

Rebecca sang on. Daisy found the bottle in the 'frig.

"God," she exclaimed as she unscrewed the top, "we're babysitting while he's downstairs making whoopee with the widow in 1 C! I wonder if she takes her pearls off when they're doing it?"

"Shh. Let her have her song, poor dear."

"I think he's picked his next wife."

"Daisy! How can you be sure?"

Rebecca sang: "Living in a fog, nothing really clear, when my time is done, who will hold me near? When I'm gone, who will remember the old days, the golden ways, all that I used to be? Who will remember me?"

I walked to her side and patted her on the shoulder.

"Rebecca, I will remember. Such a lovely song! Drink up. We have some more wine."

She looked up at me with a puzzled expression and glanced at her glass. She pushed it aside and folded her arms on the table.

"It's time for my nap now." She lay her head down. Her eyes closed.

I looked at her and murmured, "Actually, this may be one of her better days."

"Well, she's out now."

Daisy poured the Merlot into our glasses.

"Cheers," she said.

"Happy days."

We sipped.

Daisy smiled at me.

"This birthday. Ever think you'd be 85?"

"No. After Jim passed – well, you helped to keep me going."

"And you've helped me. That's what we have to do, hon. Keep on keeping on."

We sipped.

"Enough of that crap," said Daisy. "Let's look on the bright side. What are the best days you remember?"

I gave her a glance. "I don't want to be hurtful."

"It's okay. I made my own decision not to have children."

We were quiet for a moment. Daisy poured more wine.

"Okay. What about the worst day – other than your husband going."

I laughed. "That's easy. It was seventh game of the '47 World Series, when the Yankees beat the Dodgers. I cried for three days. But we got our revenge. In the '55 World Series, game seven,

Johnny Podres pitched a no-run nine innings and Brooklyn won. In Yankee Stadium!"

We sipped.

Daisy cleared her throat.

"Change of subject. What's the latest with Junior."

"You heard the noise while you were standing outside the door."

"Prince Charming at his best," she replied.

"Yes."

We sipped.

"Still trying to get you out of here, huh?"

"Yes. Jim Junior talks to me about a nice retirement home and then slips in things about professional nursing care and I have this mental picture of me tucked into bed in a sterile white room along a hallway of dozens of sterile white rooms."

"It might be a good thing – the retirement home. Some of them are called villas."

"Oh, Daisy, he and his sister are tired of feeling responsible for me. They just want to shuffle me off somewhere so I'm not a bother. Definitely not the silk glove treatment! They don't understand what this apartment means to me. My home."

"I don't understand why they think of you as a bother."

"I don't either. Maybe it's Fred."

"Junior knows about him?"

"Yes. My mistake. Sophie knows. I'm sure she told her brother."

"Okay, okay. Let's change the subject."

"Thank you. What's new with you?"

"New cleaning lady. And that restaurant down the street delivers dinners. Pretty good."

"I'll remember that."

Daisy looked at her glass. It was empty. So was mine. She reached for the bottle and we finished it off.

"Cheers."

I nodded. We drank.

Silence, broken at last by Daisy.

"You ever watch that Ellen show on television?"

"No."

"She had some female couples on last week."

"Oh?"

We sipped.

"Your daughter still living with that woman with a funny name?"

"It's a good, strong, old-fashioned name. Prudence."

"Oh. Well, are Sophie and *Prudence* living together or are they *living* together?"

"It's their business."

"Sure, sure."

She emptied her glass and twirled the stem.

"Any more wine?"

"I think there's a Pinot Grigio on the bottom shelf in the back."

Daisy rose and walked carefully to the 'frig. She rummaged on the bottom shelf and drew a bottle out. As she stood she looked at my drying rack by the sink.

"Finally did your dishes, huh?"

"I had to do something physical. Young Jim was making sarcastic comments about me on the phone to Sophie."

Daisy picked up the bottle opener she'd used before and extracted the cork with a "pop". She walked back to the table and surveyed our glasses. Hers was empty. Mine was half-full.

"Want a new glass?"

"No. Just more dishes to wash."

"I'll help."

"Thank you."

I drank the rest of mine down and gestured at the bottle.

"One more. That's it. I don't want to be stewed when Fred comes."

Daisy poured and sat down.

"Wednesday afternoons at the Orpheum they're showing Fred Astaire movies," she noted. "*Top Hat, Swing Time*. You ever see those?"

I smiled. "Mother took me when I was a little girl."

"That man could really dance! And that Ginger Rogers – boy, could she dance, too!"

I studied my glass for a moment. "They're going to get married."

"I thought they were dead!"

"No, no. My Sophie and Prudence – they're going to get married. It's legal now in New York."

"No more grandchildren!"

"For heaven's sake, Daisy, she's fifty-five." I took a swallow of the Pinot Grigio.

Daisy smiled. "Well, each to his own, the old lady said as she kissed her cow."

"I suppose so, but when it's your daughter."

"Ever meet her friend? And her friend's *daughter*."

"Several times. I've never told my son. He has strict morals."

"Oh, sure. He's figuring them out with a succession of wives."

"It wasn't like that. There were reasons."

"Back to the main topic. Sophie's significant other."

"A month or so ago, Sophie and her friend had Fred and me over for dinner. Inspection night for Fred! Prudence — Pru — cooked. It was a very nice dinner. She's younger. An artist. And she's quite a, quite a *homemaker*."

"C'mon, Lucy, it's not a dirty word. I was a homemaker after Reggie laid down the law about not shaking my legs on stage anymore. Remember my husband? Reggie went out to *work*. I went out to *play bridge*. Evenings we went out together. At least when we lived in Manhattan."

"I envy you those days. How glamorous!"

"Well, the glitzy social scene isn't all it's cracked up to be. Same boring people, same stale jokes. After we moved here I started cooking breakfast and dinner. He came home, talked about *work*. I talked about *bridge*. We were a happy twosome until the Dark Days."

I nodded. The Black Monday Crash on October 19, 1987. The mini-crash on October 13 two years later, prompted by the failed leveraged buyout of United Airlines. The junk bond market collapsed, and Reggie was very big in junk bonds.

There was a meeting of all the senior partners at his financial firm. The managing partner gave a speech. It was a brief one. That's what Reggie told Daisy when he came home early that afternoon, mimicking John, the managing partner.

"Reginald Van Horn has been a valued senior partner, yes, been with us from the beginning. But now it is a new day, um, um, significant losses, um, um, new approaches needed. Younger minds in touch with current realities."

One hour to clear out his desk. Security men walked him to the door. It was his last day of car service.

"He cried, Lucy. My husband, mind like a computer, always so full of life and keen about possibilities for the future, now he felt like a complete failure. He was sobbing. I tried to comfort him, but I was caught up in worrying about what it meant for us."

"Did you ask?"

"Yes. He had lost a great sum personally but he assured me we could continue with the same lifestyle. Mostly."

"I remember. That was when your Saturday dinners catered-in stopped. I wondered about that. And he sold the new Lincoln Town Car."

"I was in too much shock to tell you we had to—"

"You finally did, in a very quiet voice. And you asked me not to tell anyone else. I never have."

"I know. Thank you."

Daisy was quiet for a moment, staring into space.

"The awful part was that Reggie retreated into himself. He had always delighted in *Barron's,* the *Journal,* economic books, the magazines. No more. Then one day he got up, put on his suit, and told me he was going out. He'd come home at six o'clock, eat dinner, watch some television, and go to bed. I was afraid to ask him where he went.

"Not long after, I got the first telephone call. 'Mrs. Van Horn, please do something about your husband. He stands on the sidewalk across the street, looking up at our office floors. All day. It's very disruptive.'

"I didn't know what to say. The man on the other end said they'd called the police. The police said it was out of their hands because there was no law against looking. I didn't know what to do.

"Every week, the telephone calls. 'He's here again today. Down there on the street. Please do something or else we'll have to take further steps.'"

"I remember," I sympathized. "You tried so hard to get him interested in other things."

Daisy drained her glass and licked her lips.

"Wooo-ee! Did I ever. Golf, more travel, going to bars and picking up women—just kidding, just kidding. Nothing clicked with Reggie."

"But it didn't last long."

"Three months. Through the fall into winter. He'd get up, dress in his business suit, and take the subway into Manhattan. He'd be home at five and just sit in his chair until supper. All I ever heard was, 'My life is over.'

"One morning a junior partner came out of the building and told him they didn't want him hanging around anymore—it was bothering people in the office. Every time somebody looked out, there Reggie would be, standing on the sidewalk looking up. Reggie told him, 'Send John out here.'"

She paused and began to cry softly. I took a napkin from the table holder and handed it to her. Daisy dried her eyes.

"The next day, John came out and charged across the street. They argued. Reggie pulled a pistol out of his coat pocket. They wrestled. Reggie collapsed."

"I remember when you got the phone call. You came here so distraught! Absolutely beside yourself!"

"Wouldn't you be? My husband dead of a heart attack at ten in the morning on a sidewalk in Manhattan. And the gun. Scandalous. He might have killed John and all those passers by."

She put the napkin on the table and spoke fiercely. "I'm all right now. Thank you for listening. Once again."

I sighed and covered Daisy's hand with her own. "There's something about birthdays that starts you remembering that awful time."

Daisy gave me a faint smile. "It may be Rebecca and her song that stirred me up all over again."

At the mention of her name, Rebecca raised her head just above her folded arms. Now she murmured:

"Who will remember when I was in my prime. The old ways, the golden days, the way I used to be."

I patted her hand. "There, there, dear. It's all right. Go back to sleep."

Her head fell back onto her arms. Daisy took Rebecca's glass and drained it. She sighed.

"Ah, memories! A blast from the past, with a few times of di-SAS-ter."

She pushed the Pinot Grigio bottle toward me. "More?"

I covered my glass. "No thanks. I'll finish up with this."

Daisy pushed the bottle away. "I'm done."

"I suppose I'm a Pollyanna," I mused. "Always looking for a happy ending."

"We cannot go back, only forward," Daisy stated.

"The past is prologue. Who said that?"

"JFK, I think. God, what a hunk!"

"Here's to the future!" I finished off my glass. "No more pity parties for us!"

"Absolutely not! Shake."

We shook hands.

"That reminds me," said Daisy. "We haven't had 'pitter-patter' in a while. Want to test our level of—what's that word? Oh, in-e-bri-a-tion."

"Daisy, you've had too much to drink."

"If that's a challenge, you're on."

5

THE DAY AFTER ABE Weinstein took Rebecca to the neurologist, I saw him in the elevator. He looked so glum that I couldn't help myself.

"What's wrong?"

"Mrs. Scott, thank you for asking. I don't want to burden you with my problems."

"Goodness, if it's as bad as that, please tell me."

"It's Rebecca. We've been going for tests with a specialist and yesterday he told me that she's in early stage Alzheimer's or a similar type of dementia."

I was stunned. Rebecca was always such a blithe spirit. She had sung for us at Daisy and Reggie's catered Saturday dinners several times. She had a lovely voice.

"I'm sorry to hear this news" were the only words I could get out.

"He says she appears to be progressing more rapidly than most. Gave me the phone number of a support group."

Later, when I related the conversation to Daisy, she was lost in thought for a moment.

"We can't let this happen to us," she declared.

"From what I know the chances at our age are fairly slim."

She peered at me. "You have any of this in your family tree?"

"No."

"Me neither." She thought some more. "Still . . ."

"For heaven's sake, we need to be thinking about how to help Rebecca and Abe."

"We will, we will. And so will others. Hmmm . . ."

"What is it?"

"You do your crosswords every day. And the newspaper Jumbles. I play bridge. The widows down the hall from me are Scrabble addicts."

"From what I read, those are activities that help."

"Yes. But there must be something else we can do. Something together. So we can check on each other. Early signs. Are we still with it. That kind of thing."

She raised her hands. "I've got it. Silly rhymes."

"These aren't the times for that."

"See! You just did it. I said 'rhymes' and you responded with 'times.'"

"What?"

"What rhymes with 'moose'?"

"Depends on whether it's a large animal or a chocolate dessert or stuff for your hair."

"Animal."

"Goose."

"That's it. We'll call it pitter-patter. Silly name for a silly game. Only the quick witted may apply."

In this fashion our personal game was born.

Sitting at my kitchen table, saddened by my son's behavior and with Daisy caught up remembering once again the terrible events that led to Reggie's heart attack, we did silly rhymes. Who says older people can't cope!

She started.

"Do you like old age?"

"I'm happy as a sage," I responded.

"Want to have a doctor visit?"

"Personally I'd rather miss it."

Daisy had to think. "Ah, a theme!"

"Is that your dream?"

"Have you made your will yet?"

"Let's change the subject."

She persisted. "A power of attorney?"

"That's not my journey!"

Daisy smiled, "I've got a new condition."

"Another new prescription?"

"Yes. It makes me kind of woozy."

"You shouldn't get so boozy."

"Ouch." She paused, thinking. Her face lit up.

"Now I've got the hiccups."

"What? Let me turn my ears up."

Daisy frowned at me. "Lucy, I'm on the ropes."

"We're a couple of dopes," I responded.

"No, no, that's enough. Although . . ."

She thought for a moment, followed by a big grin. A stumper she would claim victory on.

"There's a new mini-camera for inner body tours . . ."

Ah. I had read about this device the day before. No difficulty with a response.

"I'll show you my polyps if you show me yours!"

We both had a big laugh.

"Okay, Lucy, I give. Too bad vaudeville's dead. We would have been great. Say, I heard an interesting story the other day. Have you heard about what happened to Edith? Lives down the block from us."

"No, what's the story?"

"She saved up a whole bunch of sleeping pills to take when things got worse."

"And?"

"Of course things got worse because that's what she was expecting."

"And?"

"Got all comfy in bed, swallowed the pills, and went to sleep. On the bed she left a letter.

"'Gone to glory.'"

"*And?*"

Daisy laughed and threw up her hands. "She woke up twelve hours later and felt so good she got out of bed, vacuumed the apartment, cooked a big breakfast and drank coffee with *caffeine*! And things went from worse to better!"

We had another big laugh.

I said, "I have a story."

"Somebody we know?"

"No. It came by way of my daughter Sophie, so you absolutely *cannot* mention it to anyone else."

"Scout's honor. Spill the beans."

"It's sad and it's funny, all at the same time."

"Please, the story!"

"Here goes. There's this older couple—"

Daisy interrupted. "As old as us?"

"I'm talking *really* old. Almost a hundred."

"And?"

"Their entire married life, they argued about everything. Only time they took a break was when she was in the hospital giving birth to their two children."

"And?"

"Their children, now well into their 60's, finally persuaded them to see a marriage counselor."

"And?"

"The counselor listened to them fighting like cats and dogs and said, 'Have you two always been like this?' They nodded 'yes.' 'For heaven's sake,' she said, 'you're both miserable. Why not get a divorce?'"

"*And?*"

"The husband and wife looked at each other and said, 'We don't want to embarrass our children. We'll wait till they die.'"

Silence. It was a jaw-dropper for Daisy.

"That's terrible!" she sputtered at last.

"Sad but true."

Daisy fingered the stem of her wine glass. "Some more wine?"

"Daisy!"

6

Two of the relationships I treasure are my friendship with Benjy Morales and Tony Alvarez. Seven-year-olds still have an innocence of heart that enables them to ask questions or say things that are considered impolite by the time they're a few years older.

On my return from the public library one Saturday morning in August I saw two youngsters sitting at opposite ends of the lobby sofa. They both had cell phones and were playing some game that prompted great hilarity.

As I passed by to the elevator, I heard them chattering in Spanish and I couldn't resist.

"Hola, niños."

They stopped and stared at me, an elderly woman with white hair who definitely did not look like someone who would speak to them in Spanish.

"Habla español?" one asked.

"Sí, un poco. Cómo estás?"

"Muy bien," replied the other youngster. The elevator door opened but I ignored it and walked closer to the two boys and spoke.

"I was a teacher of the French language for many years. So I know a little Spanish as well."

They stared.

"I'm sorry. Forgive me for interrupting."

The boy nearest me shrugged. "We're waiting for our mothers. They said to wait for them here till they get back."

"I see. My name is Lucy Scott. And what are yours?"

"I'm Benjy Morales," offered the nearest one. He gave a wave of the hand to the other.

"He's Tony Alvarez. We both live on six and we're buddies."

His friend spoke up. "Are you Haitian? You don't look Haitian."

I smiled. "No. Just a French teacher. Or I was. I live on three."

"My mom works at Bloomingdale's," stated Benjy proudly. "At the perfume counter."

"My mom doesn't need to work," piped up Tony. "My dad is an officer on the Queen Mary. He's promised me that one day I can go with him."

"Well, my dad is a banker," Benjy announced. "He has a car."

Tony sat up straighter. "My dad took me to a Yankees' game the last time he was home."

At that moment their mothers came through the door, each carrying several Trader Joe's bags. One mother shot a glance at the two youngsters.

"Boys! Don't be bothering the nice lady."

I smiled at her. "They're no bother at all. I'm Lucy Scott."

"She lives here," Tony announced.

"That's wonderful," said the other mother. "Now get up and help us with these bags!"

Benjy and Tony slid off the leather sofa and ran to help.

"Glad to meet you," said the sharp-voiced mother to me. She punched the elevator button. The door opened. Parents and children walked inside.

As the door closed Benjy gave me a big smile.

In the weeks that followed occasional ups or downs on the same elevator provided further information.

Both boys were a handful. Particularly Tony. Angie Alvarez sighed as she gave me a sixty second rundown on handling him along with the demands of her aging mother-in-law, who lived with them. She immediately apologized as she realized I was older than her husband's mother.

From elevator short takes with Rosa Morales I learned that both boys were quite bright. She had a tinkling laugh as she said, "Obviously they take after their mothers." Rosa always had a lovely scent on. I often inquired which perfume it was.

One Wednesday morning I stepped onto the elevator as she was on her way to work. She had a worried look, and I asked what was the matter.

"Oh, Mrs. Scott. I am beside myself! I'm working late and Carlos just called to say he has to stay at the bank for an important meeting at six o'clock. It's the first week of school and I haven't been able to line up our usual babysitter for Benjy. I called the Morales' but they're visiting relatives in Queens this afternoon."

"Let me help."

"Oh, thank you, but no, no, no. It is too much to ask."

I had persuaded her by the first floor. She thanked me profusely and said she would call the school so that a note would go to Benjy, telling him to come to my apartment.

"What would he like for supper?"

"He's in a macaroni and cheese phase right now. I'll have him bring down a box of Kraft's."

"Please, no need. I can fix it from what I have. Any vegetables?"

"Peas. And milk."

"Consider it done."

I walked her to the lobby door. She took my hand.

"Mrs. Scott, thank you so much! I truly appreciate this. Oh, and he'll have material for a school project in his back pack. Please nudge him to get started on it. It's due on Friday."

I opened the door for her.

"Carlos or I will be back no later than nine."

"Please, don't feel you have to rush."

"Thank you again. Oh, any problems, Benjy knows my number at work."

She rushed out the door, giving me a half wave as she turned to the left for the subway stop at the end of the block.

7

THE SAME DAY MY living room doorbell rang at four o'clock. I reminded myself to tell Benjy to use the service door if he came another time.

He stood there, backpack over one shoulder, his face an impassive mask.

"Hi, Benjy, come in."

"They told me at school that I was s'posed to come here."

"Yes, your mother and father both have to work late and Tony and his mom and grandmom had to go somewhere."

He walked past me into the living room. "Yeah, Tony said his grandmother's sister died. Queens."

"I'm sorry to hear that."

He shrugged his backpack onto my sofa. "Well, he never knew her that well. She was pretty old." He added, "Tony didn't want to go but his mom said it was a family thing."

I eyed the backpack. "Why don't you bring your backpack into the kitchen. You can sit at the table and work on your project till supper."

He picked up his backpack and followed me through the living room and into the kitchen.

"What's for supper?"

I turned and smiled at him. "Macaroni and cheese and peas."

His face brightened. "Mom tell you?"

"Yes." I turned to the table. "Okay. Backpack on one chair and you're next to it. How about a glass of milk?"

"Okay."

I went to the 'frig as he put his backpack on a chair. He didn't sit but walked over and looked at my family photo on the wall.

"Who are those people?"

"That's me and my family. Quite a while ago."

"The girl looks like my age."

"My daughter Sophie."

"How old is she now?"

"Fifty-five."

"Does she work?"

"Yes. She's a counselor in Manhattan."

"Like at school?"

"No. Separate. People who have problems come talk to her."

He studied the picture. "Is the woman you?"

"Yes."

"You're beautiful." He said it matter-of-factly. "The man is your husband?"

"Yes. Jim."

"What does he do?"

"Not much. He died many years ago."

"Oh. Who are the two boys?"

"The older one is my son, Jim Junior. We called him Little Jim. The other one is Steve."

"What do they do?"

"Little Jim works for a large company in Manhattan. The younger one, Steve, was in the Army. He was killed in a place called Iraq twelve years ago."

"Oh."

He returned to the table and sat. He began unloading his backpack. A notebook, a school primer, a small plastic bottle of Elmer's glue, colored pens, and a large bunch of popsicle sticks bundled together with a rubber band around them were laid on the table.

I put the glass of milk in front of him and sat down.

"Were you sad?"

"Sad?"

"When your son died."

"Yes. It took me a long time to get over it. That he wasn't around any more."

I had to clear my throat.

"Birthdays are the hardest. I always made a special cake for him, and every year I think, 'Time to make that cake for Steve.' And then I realize he's gone."

Benjy looked down at the materials from his backpack and began fiddling with the bunch of popsicle sticks.

"Was he smart?"

"Very."

A long silence. Benjy fiddled with the sticks. I thought about Steve.

"Mrs. Logan got all angry with Tony and me today."

"Your teacher?"

"Yeah."

He pulled the notebook closer and took a folded piece of paper out of it.

"It's not fair."

"Want to talk about it?"

"No."

He unfolded the paper. It looked like a photocopy of a sheet with three hand-drawn figures: rectangle, triangle and square.

"It was about this stupid girl in my class."

"Hmmm?"

"She's ugly."

"Benjy!"

"Well, she is. Her hair is just hacked off any which way and sometimes she smells like she forgot to take a bath."

"What's her name?"

"Molly. But me and other kids call her Pollywog."

"Hmm. What did your teacher say?"

Benjy looked at me. "Where did you teach? "

"At Jefferson Tech High School."

"Were you ever really mad at someone in your class?"

"No, they were usually pretty good."

He looked down at the table.

"Wish you were my teacher."

"High school was where I fit. Older kids."

Silence. Benjy took one of the colored pens and started drawing large x's on the sheet of paper.

He muttered, "Stupid cow."

"Benjy, that's a terrible thing to say!"

"Well, she is. When she gets called on in class, she gets stuff all mixed up and then she cries."

"Is that what happened today?"

"We were just teasing her. On the playground at recess."

I began to get the drift.

"And your teacher saw you."

"Yes. And then the bell rang and we went back inside and she gave a note to Pollywog and told her to take it to the principal's office with two other girls. Her friends. It isn't fair!"

His face flushed.

"Mrs. Logan said something."

"She came over and stood between our desks, Tony's and mine, and looked around at everybody else and said we all should be ashamed of ourselves."

"Hmm."

"We were just teasing her. Didn't mean anything by it. Most everybody does it, not just Tony and me."

"So your teacher was upset."

"She was all red in the face and —"

"Sounds terrible. I imagine you wanted to crawl under your desk."

"Yeah, But she was standing right there."

"Remember what she said?"

"No." He drew more x's on the paper. "It's not fair."

"It must have been about Polly. I mean Molly."

He took a deep breath and used it all on a very long sentence.

"She said Pollywog's father wasn't coming home because he was a soldier killed in Af-something and her mom and her were having a really tough time and she doesn't want to see or hear any of us teasing her ever again."

"Oh, my."

"And then she looked down at Tony and me and said, 'Especially you two.'"

"Oh, my, my."

He snuffled and wouldn't meet my eye.

"Some of the girls giggled."

"That didn't feel good," I commiserated.

"Stupid cows," he muttered.

"Benjy, 'stupid cows' doesn't sound like a good expression to use. Any time."

'Well, they are!"

"It's asking for more trouble. Like having to stay after school. You wouldn't like that, would you?"

"No." He drew more x's. "Can I have another glass of milk?"

"Sure thing," I said.

We never spoke about it again. When Carlos came to pick Benjy up, I told him his son had had a rough day and might want to talk about it. I never heard any more.

∽ ∽ ∽ ∽ ∽

Every other week or so Benjy would come to me after school, and sometimes Tony came with him. They both came one Monday afternoon two months after school had started.

There was a rapid knock. When I opened the door they both started speaking at once. "Wait, wait, wait," I urged. "I can't hear when you're both talking. Come in."

"Please, Mrs. Scott, you've got to help us!"

Tony joined in. "This is the most importantest thing!"

"I'll do my best, boys. Sit down and slow down. How about a glass of milk?"

A nod from each. I went to the refrigerator.

"You should have seen him!"

"It was awful!"

I poured the milk and set the glasses in front of them. I sat.

"Now, slow down and tell me what's happened."

Benjy looked at Tony.

"He's Tony's friend."

"Who is?" I asked."

"Angelo," said Tony. "And he's friends with Robbie and Andy and—"

"Whoa, now. Let's stick with Angelo. What did Angelo do?"

"Ate his breakfast in a split second!" shouted Benjy.

"Calm down. Tony, how do you know this? Were you at his house?"

"No, no, no," groaned Tony. "It's always at school."

"You have breakfast at school?"

They looked at each other. Benjy went into exaggerated patience mode.

"Everybody does. Every school day. It's free. It's a dollar and three quarters for lunch. And some kids don't have to pay for that, either."

"Okay. Free breakfasts and maybe lunch. We didn't have anything like that when I was teaching, but go on. What about Angelo?"

"He ate like this," said Tony and lifted both hands off the table and opened his mouth wide and pushed his hands at his mouth.

"And then he looked around to see if any of the grownups were watching and he says to Tony," Benjy was hopping in his seat, "'if you're my buddy, you'll give me yours.'"

"And I did," said Tony. "He was like — really hungry. And then he asked Benjy for his!"

"Our eyes were bugging out like in the cartoons," exclaimed Benjy. "And we asked him if he was okay, and he whispered that he hadn't had anything to eat since Saturday."

Tony's eyes widened. "He said his mom had a fight with her boyfriend Saturday night—"

"She kicked him out," interjected Benjy.

'And then she got some clothes together and took the baby and left." Tony continued. "All there was in the house was a can of beans, a couple of hot dogs and milk for the baby. So he ate that, and couldn't find any money around, so that was it till he came to school today."

Benjy spoke up. "He was dozing on and off. But he sits behind me and I kept moving in my seat and he'd wake up so Mrs. Logan didn't see how tired he was."

"Besides," said Tony, "lots of kids are sleepy on Monday."

"At recess we got the whole story," Benjy went on. "Then at lunch we asked him what he was going to do and he said, 'go back home and see if Mom and the kid are there.'"

"I had a dollar more than my lunch money and I gave it to him for supper," explained Tony, who had a worried look on his face. "Doesn't seem like much."

"What a sad story," I exclaimed. "You both were very good friends to help him."

"He doesn't want anybody to know," Tony said.

"So when we waited around after class to talk to Mrs. Logan, we used a 'nonymous name," Benjy chimed in.

"That was very brave of both of you. To speak to your teacher. What did she say?"

"She got all concerned, and wanted to know more but we didn't want to rat on Angelo," Tony said. "Nobody likes a ratter."

"Is that the end of it, then?"

"No!" Benjy's excitement was mounting again. "She gave Tony a piece of paper with the school number and told him to ask his mother to call between four and five today."

Tony broke in, "But my mom is gone to her sister's today, and this is urgent!"

"Yes! Super urgent!" shouted Benjy. "That's why we want *you* to call." He looked at the kitchen wall clock as Tony thrust a piece of paper at me. "Not much time. Hurry!"

"Boys, boys! I hear your concern but I can't call up your teacher and pretend I'm Tony's mother."

Silence. They were both in deep thought.

"Okay," Benjy burst forth, "it's like a TV show I saw last week. You're 'an interested party.' That's what you tell her. No names."

They both looked at me so expectantly that I almost laughed.

"All right. I won't do that but I will call. Let me go get my phone."

They followed me into the living room and sat on the edge of the sofa. I sat in my recliner and picked up the hand-held phone from its base. I looked at the note and dialed.

The school office answered. I said I'd been told I could reach Mrs. Logan at this number.

I was put on hold. Benjy and Tony started wiggling on the sofa.

"Hello."

"Mrs. Logan?"

"Yes. Who's this?"

"I'm calling about a boy whose mother has abandoned him. He needs help."

"Angelo?"

"Yes."

"You're Tony's mother."

"His mother isn't able to call today. I'm a friend. Tony is quite upset."

"It's a very upsetting situation. His mother has walked out before for several weeks. Angelo has been taken under care on those occasions, and I have a call into Social Services on an emergency basis."

"No relatives he could go to?"

"An aunt who lives in the Bronx. We try to keep things more local so he can maintain his school connection. That's about the only stable thing in his life."

"I see. What about food?"

A sigh on the other end. "If Social Services acts soon, he'll be in a place where a full supper is served."

"Tony is concerned about this evening. Food for Angelo."

"I have his cell number. I'll call as I leave school to learn if his mother has returned home."

"And if she hasn't?"

"There's not much I can do. I hope he has food in the apartment or he has helpful neighbors. I'm sorry."

"Hold on a minute." I held my hand over the mouthpiece and looked at Tony.

"Do you know where he lives?"

Tony nodded.

"Very far from here?"

"Couple of blocks."

"Mrs. Logan, we may have the immediate need covered from here."

"Oh, I'm so glad. Angelo is really a nice boy." She sighed. "One of several children who have incredible home situations. I appreciate your help."

"Glad to do it."

"And what is your name, please?"

"Lucy. I am an interested party."

I could tell she was smiling on the other end. "I see. A friend of Tony and Benjy."

"Yes, you might say that."

"While you're on the line, let me mention one other thing."

"Yes?"

"The school provides breakfast, and, for students in Angelo's circumstances, lunch is free. But the weekends are a problem for many of our children. Last school year there was a mother who headed up a program to make weekend food packs for certain children to take home on Friday so they'd be sure to have nutritious food."

"I see."

"I regret to say that in our school there is no reimbursement for food costs, but she found area grocers who were willing to help and that kept expenses down."

"Hmm."

"Lucy, your interest in Angelo shows you may be just the person to head this up for the second graders."

"I need to think about this. I have a number of involvements already."

"That's good to hear. But the food pack program has tangible results. I'd like to talk with you further about it."

"Surely. I have to go now. I can reach you at this number?"

"Yes. Except for Fridays, I am usually around until five."

"Very well."

"And thank you! We need all the 'interested parties' we can get! 'Bye now."

I placed the phone back on its charging stand.

Tony and Benjy were looking at me with awe-filled eyes.

"You are wonderfulest!" Tony said.

Benjy gave him a mock punch on the chest. "Told you," he said.

"One more thing," said I. "Tony, you have Angelo's cell number?"

"Yeah."

"Dial it and find out how he's doing. If he needs food I'll be glad to walk you two over to give him some money."

We did.

༄ ༄ ༄ ༄ ༄

There was another time that is so very special to me. It happened one evening not long after the Angelo episode. About eight o'clock, Rosa called.

"Mrs. Scott, Benjy is on his way down to see you. I hope it's not inconvenient?"

"Just sitting here reading a book."

"Send him back up when he's talked to you."

"Will do," I replied. I heard the hall stairway door clang shut and immediately after a knock on my service door. I hurried and opened it. Benjy rushed in.

"Mrs. Scott, I want you to do the biggest favor anybody ever asked for!"

"Whoa, Benjy. Come here and talk to me."

We both sat at the kitchen table.

"Now. Slow down and tell me what this is about."

"You've got to help me. Please."

"Help you with what?"

"This Friday at school is Grandparents' Day."

"Oh?"

"I don't have a grandparent," he wailed. "All the other kids do. Even Tony. She grumbled but said she would go."

"Calm down, Benjy. I think I understand but you tell me what you want me to do."

"Pretend you're my grandmother!"

"Let me think a moment."

I thought.

"Okay. Listen to me. I can't pretend to be your grandmother. That's like lying."

His face fell. I smiled.

"But I'm sure no one would object if I came as your grandfriend."

He looked puzzled, then beamed at me. "Yes! My grand-friend! Oh, and you're supposed to bring a treat."

"How about brownies?"

"Yes. My grandfriend and brownies."

He stood up and gave me a big hug.

"I've got to go tell Mom now. 'Bye."

He was out the door and I heard the stairwell door clang shut again as he raced up to six.

Dear, dear Benjy.

My role as Grandfriend on Friday at his school was quite successful.

8

My reminiscing about Benjy and Tony carried me through a monologue by Daisy about her new favorite casserole. She was interrupted by a sudden knock on the door, and I came back to earth.

"Oh, oh." I rose. "There's Rebecca's husband."

Daisy snorted. "Must have been a quickie."

"Oh, Daisy! I hear she has a Steinway. And I've heard him sing."

"That's right. They make beautiful music together."

I opened the door as Daisy unlocked the wheels on Rebecca's chair.

"Lucy, thank you so much for your help," Abe said.

"It's a privilege. Truly."

He nodded at Daisy. "Hello, Mrs. Van Horn."

Rebecca stirred as her husband took the handles of the wheel chair. Abe was looking at me.

"I understand you may be leaving us soon."

"It seems so. My children are determined to get me into a nursing home. I don't understand. I'm not ready for it. I can take care of myself, and all my friends are here."

"What a pity. I've never met your son and daughter. They were quite grown and on their own when Rebecca and I moved in. Is there no alternative?"

"My son is tired of feeling responsible for me. My son Jim, the big corporate executive. I call him Boom-Boom. Boom! Make this decision! Boom! Make that decision!"

Abe smiled. "I've read about him in the business pages. Looks like he's in line to be the next president of his company."

Daisy spoke up. "You're a lawyer. Can she sue her children for elder abuse?"

"I don't think that fits this situation," Abe replied. "At any rate, I dealt in real estate."

I nodded. "Yes. Do you miss going in to the office?"

"My partners are quite capable. Besides, the last few years . . ." He gestured at Rebecca.

"She's a dear." I smiled at her. "She even had a glass of wine with us to celebrate my birthday."

As Abe pushed the wheel chair out the door I held open, Rebecca lifted her head and peered at me. "Happy Birthday, Daisy."

Abe patted her shoulder. "Lucy, darling." He looked at me. "May you enjoy many more."

"Thank you." I closed the door. "He certainly is a handsome fellow."

Daisy gave me one of her cheesy smiles.

"Seems to get enough exercise, that's for sure!"

I moved back to the table. Four knocks at the door, firm but not loud.

Daisy's smile subsided to normal as she moved toward the door.

"I'll bet that's Fred. Now *he's* my kind of man."

It wasn't Fred. "Oh, Mr. K!"

Mr. K is an assistant at the pharmacy where my prescriptions are registered.

He's enrolled in a program for a professional degree in pharmacy. He's told me that he figures he can do it in four or five years and graduate debt-free. I would gladly offer funding to help him complete his pharmacy degree more quickly, but I have not. The way he carries himself tells me that his mother schooled him in standing on his own two feet, accepting charitable help from no one.

He stood in the doorway carrying a white paper sack. He handed it to Daisy and called to me.

"Hi, Professor Scott. Your prescriptions. When you put them in your pillbox, remember: morning pills on the blue side; evening pills on the red. You have another visitor right behind me. 'Bye now."

As he left we heard Fred's voice. "Is the birthday girl in?"

Mr. K called back from the hallway. "Oh. *Bon anniversaire*, Professor."

Daisy beamed. "Come on in, Prince Charming. She's been waiting for you."

"Daisy!" Honestly, sometimes she is just too much.

Fred stepped in with a bouquet of yellow roses, my favorite, in one hand and a bottle of champagne in the other. He waved the bottle at me.

"Real French champagne! No expense spared for this occasion!"

Daisy tittered.

"Well, three's a crowd, so I'm out of here. Have fun!"

9

Daisy moved around Fred and exited, smiling broadly and waving at me behind his back.

I took the flowers as Fred deposited the champagne on the table.

"Fred, how sweet. Let me get a vase."

I started to turn but he put a hand on my shoulder.

"Just one kiss first?"

I gave him a peck on the cheek. He feigned disappointment.

"I was hoping for more."

"What did you have in mind?"

"How about a kiss for every birthday? That ought to cover the subject."

"Oh, Fred." I walked into the kitchen and found a vase, made a nice arrangement of the yellow roses, and looked over my shoulder. He was still standing.

"Please. Sit."

"One more kiss."

I returned to the table and put the vase down.

"They're lovely flowers. Thank you."

"I'm not looking at the flowers."

He put his arms around me. We had a long, passionate kiss until I ran out of breath and leaned away.

"That's it. One."

"Lucy, darling, marry me!"

"Oh, Fred, we've been over this before! Please, sit down."

"Lucy, darling, with you each morning is a bright new day."

Fred always was such a romantic. Positively turns a girl's head. But one must be realistic.

"We've done some talking about this before," he pleaded. "Your birthday's a good time to talk some more. We're not getting younger and I'm hoping today is the day you'll say we'll marry."

"Thank you," I said firmly, "but no. I think a little distance is what helps us to get along so well. You're up in 4 B. I'm down here on 3."

"Let's merge. There's a vacancy, 5 C. Three bedrooms. Same layout as yours, but new surroundings for both of us."

"Don't be silly. You know I'll always be here for you. But day-in, day-out togetherness? That would cure your romantic notions in a week!"

He looked me up and down. "*My* notions? What did you have in mind, our Lady of the Bathrobe?"

"Oh, Fred! I would have dressed, but after a lovely soak in the tub my son came. A surprise visit and we had a very unpleasant conversation. Then Daisy arrived and she had her annual Memory of Times Past. Then Rebecca. I'm all clean but I didn't have time to change."

He knelt and took my hand.

"Lucy, marry me. We'll make a great couple."

"Goodness, we're too old for this! Here, let me help you up."

He put one hand on the table and I pulled the other. He stood.

"And furthermore," I said to him, "you should know I won't let you go, but our families don't want us to be more than just friends, you and me."

"Lucy, it's *our* lives. You know my daughter approves. My son —well, he's out in California."

I shook my head. "Fred, you know I'm yours already. Don't complicate matters."

He smiled.

"I wrote another poem today about us.

"'Each day a new morning, like a gift from above. A day you could spend making memories with someone you love.'"

"Thank you, Fred."

"I thought you might put it into French and we could make it a song. Our duet."

I gave him a peck on the cheek. "We're older and wiser, why can't that be enough?"

He grinned. "No more arguments today. It's your birthday, and I have a special present for you."

"Hmm." I knew about his 'special presents.' "And what might that be?"

"First, one more kiss to send away the arguing."

"What argu—mmph."

At last he released me. We looked at each other. He took my hand and gave me a twirl towards the hallway door that led to the bedroom. He deftly opened the door, twirled me through it and closed the door gently behind him, saying as he did so, "*Je t'aime, mon amour.*"

All I will say is that the next thirty minutes were quite pleasurable. For once I didn't bottle it up inside for the sake of my neighbors but exploded with several loud "Yips!"

We lay there, holding each other as we cooled down.

And then came the climax of my day. I heard the voice of my son from the kitchen.

"Mom? I'm here."

"Good God!" Fred exclaimed softly. "Is that your son?"

We hugged each other more tightly.

"Sounds like it," I whispered. "Maybe he'll go away."

A moment of quiet.

"Mom? Are you all right?"

We lay still. Fred said, "You need a lock on your bedroom door."

I sat up. "He has his own agenda today. Me. I better go."

A louder call from the kitchen. "Mother?"

I picked my bathrobe up from the floor and shrugged into it.

"Fred, I'm sorry."

"Send him away and come back."

I didn't answer.

I carefully closed the bedroom door behind me and entered the kitchen while pulling my bathrobe cord around me tight.

I regarded my son. "Oh. You."

"I heard a sound. Are you all right?"

"Just doing my afternoon exercises. Keeping myself limber."

He was staring at me. I let loose a loud "Yip!"

"Oh!" He was startled and took a step back.

"*Mon amant est ici. Un homme de grande passion.*"

"Yes, yes. Why do you always launch into French at serious moments!"

He gestured at the table.

"I spent the afternoon looking out for your future. These are brochures from three affordable places. Choose one."

He paused and looked away from me. "Sis agrees. I'll be back from London in two weeks."

"Two weeks! How can I decide in two weeks! I don't agree with any of this."

"Mom. I heard your viewpoint earlier this afternoon. You weren't listening to me. It's for your own good."

He looked at me. My son.

"I've had to pull a few strings to get you considered by any of these places."

"Considered!"

"Yes, Mom. Pulling strings is what I'm good at."

He glanced at his watch. "Gotta go."

"Then go."

I crossed my arms across my chest and gave him an icy glare.

He shrugged, picked up his briefcase off the table, and with his other hand he lifted the champagne for a look.

"Huh, French. Very nice, Mom. Enjoy."

He put the bottle down and gestured at the three brochures.

"Pick one. We'll go visit the one you like when I'm back."

"I know what I like," I snapped. "And none of those places are it. This is my home."

"Look, don't be difficult." His voice rose. "I've spent too much of my time on it already. Choose the furniture you want to take with you."

"Choose furniture!"

"Time to downsize, Mom." He started edging toward the door. "Only one bedroom, small living room—your table can fit in there—and a walk-in kitchen."

"But what about all my friends here?"

"They can visit."

He didn't look back and slammed the door on his way out.

I walked over to the table and picked up a brochure. Looked at it in all its glossy promotional beauty.

"*Merde!*"

The hall door opened and Fred emerged.

"Sonny boy gone?"

He was stuffing his shirt into his trousers and zipping up.

"What are you doing?" I asked.

"I couldn't help but hear the conversation. Figured you'd be too upset for more loving."

He was barefoot. I pointed at his feet and laughed.

"Lucy, I'm glad you still have a sense of humor."

"Oh, Fred. It's terrible. Even ruins our love life. He might as well lock me up and throw away the key!"

Fred, darling Fred, came and gave me a hug. I hugged back.

"'Two weeks to choose,' he said. Brought brochures. 'Pick one,' he said. 'Time to downsize.' Oh, Fred, what am I going to do?"

He hugged me tighter. "We'll do something, sweetheart. We'll figure something out." He smiled. "We could be married by the time he gets back."

"No, no, no," I wailed. "You don't know my son. He'd figure out a way to get around that and I'd be in one place and you'd still be here!"

Fred pulled back and looked and gave me a fierce look.

"Never, ever."

10

I MET FRED A year before. I was in the Brooklyn Public Library stacks hunting for a large-print Elizabeth George novel. It was on the highest shelf and I had to reach a little. When I pulled it out, I was not ready for the heft of it and it slipped out of my fingers and fell to the floor.

As I bent to retrieve it, a man's hand slid under mine and said, "Here, let me."

"No, I can get it."

We stood, both holding an edge of the book. He released his grasp and smiled at me, "All yours."

Dear God, I felt an instant rush of emotion. The years dropped away. "All yours," was what Jim said to me as he reached a climax in our lovemaking. I closed my eyes.

When I opened them, the stranger was still there, concerned. "Are you all right?"

I steadied myself against a shelf and stammered out my thanks.

"Need to sit down? There's a chair just around the corner."

Embarrassed, I looked away. "I wasn't prepared for such a heavy book."

He smiled and his blue eyes sparkled. "I know. These large-print editions can be pretty daunting." He cleared his throat and looked over his shoulder. "I was looking for a P. D. James, myself."

He glanced at my book title. "Good luck. I found that one pretty hard going. Plots, subplots and sub-subplots. Wore me out."

"Yes, her later books are like that."

He looked at me and smiled again. "Well, have a nice read."

I managed to pull myself together and made it to the end of the stack without looking back. But his image stuck in my mind. He was bald on top. He had a kind, lined face that indicated he was around my age. And I had noticed he wore no wedding ring.

Don't be silly, I scolded myself.

I checked the book out and thought no more of the stranger until I was walking up the library steps two weeks later. I felt a flutter in my chest.

I wonder if he'll be here?

Oh, come on, I crossly told myself. Nevertheless, I sneaked a glance here and there as I entered. And then I saw him.

Just beyond the book and materials return point there was a long row of high narrow tables and atop them a dozen or more computers.

He was typing something and paused, his brow furrowed in concentration.

I stood still. He glanced my way and saw me. His face lit up and he gave me a smile and a little wave before his gaze returned to the computer screen.

I plopped my book down on the returns desk and fled.

That night I tossed and turned on my bed.

Why am I thinking about it? I asked myself. *Get over it.*

My Self responded. *What are you afraid of?*

What, me afraid?

You've had your guard up against men for all these years.

What if—

Oh, for heaven's sake, I'm an old woman with a lined face and a body that's definitely not slim anymore. Who would be interested in me!

Oh, thinking about the possibility?

Of course not!

Looks to be about your age. Hmm?

He's not my type.

Oh, you have a type now?

He's bald on top and—

But he genuinely cared. You saw it in his eyes.

I am not *interested!*

Liar, liar, pants on fire!

I thumped a pillow and turned to a new position. I finally fell asleep around three a.m.

The next day it rained heavily. It was a dour, grim day. I thought about the years that had led me to this time of old age. I had a new understanding and sympathy for elderly women who decided on suicide. Meaningless, lonely lives. Better to end it all.

The next morning the storm had passed. It was a beautiful blue-sky day, filled with possibilities. I hummed as I vacuumed my area rugs. I dusted the plaques in Jim's memorabilia room and the files of Little Jim's news clippings of one business success after another. Even Sophie's high school and college yearbooks and her Pooh Bear got a swipe of the cloth. I sang along to the sound track of *La Vie en Rose* turned up high on my living room stereo. I thought of ways to make things better between me and Little Jim and Sophie.

Then, pleasantly tired, I sat at my kitchen table sipping a glass of Merlot and thought, *Why not?*

In the same instant, I knew why not. What I'd heard at a program of the Widows' Club many years before.

Younger readers: If you cannot remember what life was like before cell phones, Facebook, texting, twitter, and tweets, pass over the next two chapters. My account of life as it used to be will bore you.

11

THE WOMEN GATHERED IN the church's atrium before worship every Sunday. The Widows' Club. They sat on comfortable sofas and chairs as I walked by them on my way into the sanctuary. I imagined them to have humorless, meaningless lives, passing through their remaining earthly hours until they could rejoin their spouses in whatever chapter comes next.

One day I had a telephone call from one of their members.

"Lucy Scott?"

"Speaking."

"My name is Carolyn Baker. I'm a member of Asbury Church. I sit with a group of members in the atrium before worship. We've seen you walking by."

"Ah. The Widows' Club."

A throaty laugh came down the line. "Yes, we know about our label, but we actually call ourselves the Lively Ladies. We're an informal support group for each other and a whole lot more."

"How nice."

"Pastor Roger spoke to me last week and mentioned that you might be ready to join us in some of our activities."

I thought of knitting groups, recipe swapping, tales of the "good old days" and banal conversations.

"Thank you, but I am not interested."

"That's often the first reaction. I just want to tell you of an opportunity that's coming up. We're getting together a party to go to a Wednesday matinee in Manhattan next month to see *Cats*, Andrew Lloyd Webber's new musical."

"Oh." Daisy and I already had tickets for an earlier date.

"Wanted you to know. If you're interested, please call me by Thursday noon."

"Thank you, Carolyn. I'll think about it."

"Thursday noon is the deadline."

"Uh huh. Thursday at noon."

"I'll give you my number." She recited it twice.

"Got it. Thank you."

"My pleasure. Hope you can come with us. Bye now. 'Bye."

I passed on the first invitation as well as the next dozen.

A year later, C. C. was more assertive. She stepped into my path as I was crossing the atrium.

"Hello, Lucy. I'm C.C. Hutchinson."

She was an attractive heavyset woman with an authoritative manner.

"I'll only take a minute. We all want to hear Pastor Roger's sermon on Mary Magdalene today. He is *such* a Bible scholar yet he is able to make it all understandable to us."

"Yes." I could only agree.

"The Lively Ladies are having a special meeting this Thursday afternoon at Lily Paines' apartment."

She gestured toward the group gathered on chairs and the sofa. A slim gray-haired woman beamed at me and gave a little wave. She looked vaguely familiar.

"Lily lives in your building, The Russell House."

"Ah."

"We have a guest speaker, a psychologist, whose topic will be 'What to Watch Out for in Dating and Mating.'"

I could not repress a smile. "Thank you, but I really am not interested."

"I understand. You are still grieving."

I stood up straighter. The nerve!

She smiled. "Please, you're taking what I said as an insult. But all of us," another gesture toward the group, "have gone through this process and then we started living again."

It's hard to be polite while speaking with an icy tone, but I tried.

"Thank you very much. Now if you'll excuse me, I'm going into worship."

12

IN THE END I went, if only to forestall the tenacious Lily in 2 D from further calls. She knocked on my door Monday morning, Tuesday afternoon, and Wednesday evening to remind me of the important meeting on Thursday. Each time she ended her sales pitch with the same clincher.

"Dr. Parker is an expert on the subject. For your own protection, you need to come hear her."

I arrived late. Extra folding chairs had been brought into the living room, and only two were empty. I chose one in the row of folding chairs behind the sofa, which had been pulled forward. The eleven other women present were balancing tea cups, cookies, and lace napkins on their laps while chatting.

C.C. gave me a broad smile, "Ladies, ladies. Our newest member also lives here. I introduce to you, Lucy Scott."

There were murmurs of welcome and a warm glow in my direction from Lily, who rose and began a circuit of retrieving tea cups.

One woman, obviously interrupted by my arrival, stated her view loudly.

"I still think Lovely Ladies is a silly name. Why not the 'Brooklyn Bombshells' or something else that's more dramatic. After all, we don't sit at home twiddling our thumbs!"

"Good point, Elsie," C.C. noted. "Let's think about a better name for discussion at our next meeting." A glance at me. "Lucy, if you don't mind, I'll introduce our speaker now and afterwards we'll all introduce ourselves and tell you a bit about our lives."

I nodded and she turned to a woman who looked to be in her early 50s.

"Dr. Parker is noted for her work with the elderly, particularly in the area of post-spousal relationships. She holds degrees from Columbia University and the University of Chicago. She has told me that she is happily married to her husband of twenty-five years, who teaches at City College. They have three grown children. Dr. Parker."

"Thank you, Mrs. Hutchinson." Her eyes circled the group. "Using one's married name is the start of my conversation with you. How do you wish to be introduced in settings in which eligible men may be present? You may already have settled the issue, but the name we choose to be known by initially in more formal situations is important."

She smiled at C.C. "C.C. has kindly given me her permission to use the name she goes by with friends."

"What's a formal situation?" asked one of the women.

"One in which you expect to be respected, even when your friends introduce you to a male they see as a potential match. In a conversation with that person, you may then say something like, 'Please call be Ellie.' That's my name among friends."

"Just don't call me 'Cougar,'" murmured another woman.

"Exactly." Ellie Parker looked around the group. "Are you others familiar with the term 'Cougar'?"

Several nods outnumbered by headshakes.

"Well, then, let's talk about the competition. 'Cougar' is a slang word for a divorcee or widow who is on the prowl for a man, usually wealthy, who will support her in the style to which she was accustomed. Or it could be a person who has a degree of fame, which she can ride on.

"A second term is applied to women who believe the way to a man's heart is through his stomach. They are called 'Casserole Mamas' or 'Casserole Queens.' Such women usually know the male they are interested in. His spouse has died or he was divorced at a later age. Poor fellow, be he a pastor, plumber or whatever. What would be better than good, home cooked food to promote one's credentials and availability to a lonely man."

"Didn't work out for me," muttered a woman with a robust figure. "Old goat wanted someone younger."

"Yes, that's a peril. Sometimes it works and sometimes it doesn't. If you are not in that mode, it still helps to know that both Cougars and Casserole Queens may be on the prowl for your man.

There are several other terms, and we'll talk about them later. But now let me move on to the subject of dating and possibly marrying."

"I've been married three times," said another woman, silver haired. "Outlived them all."

"I hope you were the chief beneficiary," smiled Ellie Parker.

"Absolutely. The last two had to establish joint bank accounts and draw up new wills before we said 'I do.'" She cast a proud glance at the others.

Ellie Parker continued. "That brings up several other issues that need to be considered before marriage. Not just joint bank accounts and new wills, but also social security, health benefits, the wariness or anger expressed by the male's child or children toward you. Or your own children may feel threatened by a new male on the scene.

"If possible, you and your man will need to reassure grown children on both sides of your continuing love for them and ask for their understanding of your new happiness.

"Some couples maintain a loving relationship but prefer to keep their own system intact. I've counseled some who didn't marry and continued to live in their respective houses while enjoying periodic nights together."

"We had separate bedrooms," noted the woman of three husbands.

"Yes, that's often an option also. Married or not married but living together with separate space. Helps to make nights together more special. But now, let's go back to the beginning of it all.

"Let's say you have met someone at a party, a Bar Mitzvah, at the theater, or a funeral—"

The room rocked with laughter. She smiled.

"I know. It may sound silly, but what is the main activity for many of us as we age? We go to funerals, or at least the visitation."

Murmurs of agreement.

"Whatever the place where you meet, something interests you about the other person. The way he's dressed, the way he speaks, the glance he gives you, a brief conversation, whatever. And it seems that, just possibly, he might be interested in you."

"I met my second husband at the Leisure Time Bowling Alley next to the Port Authority," piped up the silver-haired lady.

Ellie Parker smiled. "That's the point. Go to settings where you'll meet people with similar interests to yours. Church, sporting events, dinner with friends and their friends, movies, Broadway shows, bowling alleys—"

"We had some great times," silver hair interjected. "He always wanted a perfect game. Played forty years and never a perfect game.

"Then one Saturday afternoon, he made it. Strike after strike. People started drifting over to his alley. A perfect game.

"He started jumping up and down and shouting and then he went all red in the face and keeled over. Massive coronary."

We all stared at her. She sat back in her chair and smiled.

"My, goodness," C.C. said brightly, "what an experience, Sara. Now let's hold our comments until Dr. Parker is finished. Ellie?"

"I'll move on to a more modern connection. Places such as personal columns in newspapers and magazines. Marriages do result from such contacts on occasion. If you engage in such contacts, please remember to *always* meet in a neutral setting where other people are around."

A woman who had not spoken before leaned forward.

"I tried that one time. We exchanged photos. When we met, he didn't look like his picture!" She laughed. "But then, I didn't either."

Ellie Parker nodded. "Quite so. Honest presentations by both parties helps.

"The other thing to beware of is men who simply want to be taken care of—with your money. Have you heard of the phrase 'a nurse and a purse' to describe what some older men are looking for?"

There were murmurs of agreement.

"But let's go back to basics. Let's assume it has been awhile since you've dated. Now think with me about a possible second contact. You have met him somewhere previously. There was a spark of interest shown by him that intrigued you. It stopped there. You're home now, thinking about it. You've grown up in an age in which a lady waits for the man to make the next move. Unfortunately, days pass and you don't hear from him. What to do?

"It depends on whether or not you were with friends and he was part of the company. You might ask them to convey a message saying you enjoyed meeting him. Or if they have an address you might drop a brief note to him that says the same thing. If you were solo when you first met and are really eager, it depends on how much initiative you wish to take. Perhaps you write your phone number on a matchbook and slip it to him, or he to you. That still seems overly forward for people our age, but it is done."

She smiled. "Just remember. First meeting, or second or third: public place. Be wise with guys and avoid compromising situations."

Ellie Parker went on to other aspects of dating and mating. She eventually concluded and questions were in order. I had had enough. I rose as quietly as possible.

"Thank you all," a look at my watch, "but I have another engagement."

In the elevator ascending to my floor, I decided that was my first and last time at a gathering of the Widows' Club.

Tears filled my eyes. What I wanted was to have Jim back. I knew that wasn't possible. I would continue to explore ways to keep myself busy and engaged with others. But I absolutely, positively had no desire for 'dating and mating' anyone. My wedding ring was firmly fixed on my finger!

13

MY USUAL ROUTINE OF activities precluded much thinking about the man I'd met at the library. I had added a Saturday afternoon tutoring program at the church to assist high school students who needed help with French. The program required serious prep time during the week for me.

As I look back at myself a year ago, I have to laugh. In hindsight it is clear I was keeping busy so as not to get my hopes up over chance meetings in the library. Yes, I went to return books and check out new ones. No sign of the helpful stranger.

And then, on a day forever to be engraved in my memory, he called. November 1st of last year. I glanced at the grandfather clock in the corner as I put my Elizabeth George novel down. Seven thirty-five in the evening.

"Lucy Scott, please."

"If this is a telephone solicitation, I'm not interested!"

There was a pause and then a burst of laughter.

"Mrs. Scott, I'm Fred Jorgensen. We met at the library. I helped you with the large-print book that fell off the shelf. I simply wanted to give you a ring."

"Oh." My turn to pause. "How did you get my name and number?"

"It wasn't easy! I told one of the people at the Return Desk that I was interested in a lovely woman who frequents the library. When I described you, she knew right away who it was and told me your name. You are well known at The Brooklyn Public Library."

"Yes, but my telephone number? It's unlisted."

"Actually, my informant had you as a French teacher years ago. I did some research on faculty records and updates, family, that kind of thing."

"My goodness!"

"Indeed."

"How were you able to do all that?"

"The short answer is that my career life was spent in electronics. There are ways. But I am so glad to reach you. I've been looking for you at the library for almost a month now."

"You have?" *Oh, stupid remark. Stupid, stupid, stupid.*

"Sure enough. If I know when you'll be there, I'll treat for coffee and muffins at the café down the street. We can discuss contemporary crime novels."

"Oh. I'll have to ask my husband—"

Another gust of laughter.

"Please. I know better. Your husband James passed away some time ago. If you don't want to meet me, just say so. As for me, I have been remembering the touch of your warm hand."

I was silent. *What a come-on line. I wonder how many others he's tried that one on?* "Lucy?"

What can it hurt?

"I'm sorry, I'm just a bit flustered. A discussion over coffee and muffins sounds wonderful."

"Okay. Skip the library. Next Friday at two? The lunch crowd should have dissipated by then."

"Friday's not good for me. Thursday?"

"Okay. I'll meet you at the café. Thursday at two. Goodbye for now."

14

I HAD SEVERAL DAYS to think about meeting Fred. I was interested and disinterested at the same time. *Why not?* warred with *Am I a sucker for a smooth line or what?* Vague recollections of Ellie Parker's warnings so long ago kept rising up in my mind. *But it's a neutral place. Nothing ventured, nothing gained.*

The day arrived. I put on a simple blouse and skirt outfit and my pearls.

I did not want to be the first to arrive lest I seem overly eager. Nor did I wish to be seen as one of those women who is always late. I compromised and opened the café door precisely at five minutes after two on Thursday.

There were a dozen tables in the small room. Four were filled with patrons finishing their lunches. Fred was seated at a table near the café's register. He was speaking to a woman standing nearby She was too nicely dressed to be a waitress. I judged her to be about fifty years old.

What have we here? I wondered. *Perhaps the owner?*

Fred saw me and stood, smiling. He said a few more words to the woman, who had turned to see me. She had a speculative gaze that vanished as she walked across the room to another table where a cup of coffee and a croissant were placed.

Fred held out both his hands. "Lucy, I am so glad to see you! Come sit down."

We sat.

"Ah, a glorious moment," he murmured. "The coffee is very good, and I recommend the chocolate croissants, freshly baked within the hour."

"That's fine."

"Cream, sugar?"

"Cream only, please."

He turned and called to the man at the register. "Jorge, two coffees, cream only, and two chocolate croissants."

He turned to me. "Return any mysteries today?"

"No. Just came straight here."

"Oh, good."

Jorge brought the coffee and croissants. My host thanked him.

We stirred the coffee in our cups, both of us looking down at the vinyl table top. He looked up and broke the silence.

"Okay. You don't know much about me and I don't know much about you. What I propose is that we skip the book discussion and instead tell each other a little bit about our lives."

"I'm not sure I want to do that."

"Lucy, Lucy, Lucy. Whenever we see each other in the library, we'll at least know a bit about the person we are waving to."

"Why do you want to go through all this with me?"

He sighed. "A thousand women would be jumping at—"

"Well, then, why not call one of them up?"

He looked away. "If I really tell you why I wanted us to get together, you'll laugh."

"Try me."

"That day—that day in the library when we both reached for the book and raised it up."

He swallowed and his gaze turned back to me. "What I saw was a woman with a lovely face and intelligent eyes without guile."

"No guile?"

"Openness, not calculating. Well, a little embarrassed also."

We both looked down and stirred our cups. And I will never understand why I said the first thing that popped into my head.

"Of course I have intelligent eyes. I was high school valedictorian."

He stared. "Really?"

"And on the Dean's list through college, which wasn't easy in mostly night school *and* minding three young children during the day."

"You were valedictorian?"

"Yes. And Phi Beta Kappa in college."

He gave me a big grin. "Me, too."

"You, too, what?"

"High school valedictorian and Phi Beta Kappa." He paused. "High school graduation, did you give a speech?"

"Something. All I remember is that I ended by inviting everyone to join me in whistling the school's fight song."

"Mine was about the importance of *pi*," he murmured.

"Pi?"

"You know, 3.14 forever."

"I studied French."

"Surely you had some math."

"Nothing that stuck."

Fred stirred his coffee again. "So we can call each other 'Val.' What about a little more information?"

I thought about it.

"All right." I smiled. "Short biographies."

"Good. You first."

"You already know about me. You first."

"My knowledge of you is quite limited, but all right, I'll go first." His eyes twinkled. "Stop me if this is boring."

He paused and thought before he started in.

"My full name is Niels Frederik Jorgensen. Frederik with no 'c' and a 'k' on the end. My mother has told me that I was conceived on board a ship from Denmark to New York late in 1933. I was born on July 10, 1934. My father was a physicist who studied under Niels Bohr at the University of Copenhagen. My father saw which way the wind was blowing in Germany, the nation south of Denmark. He chose to emigrate to the U.S. I was born later that year and my first name was given me in tribute to Bohr."

He paused.

"Lucy, you look like you're about to burst into laughter. Is my background that funny?"

"Sorry," I said, and reached for his hand. "It's such an amazing coincidence."

"Don't tell me you're Danish, too?"

"No, no." And then I really did let loose with laughter. Fred drew his hand back and had a bewildered expression.

I used a napkin to dry my eyes. "It's nothing about you. July the tenth was Calvin's birthday."

"I thought your husband's name was James?"

"Yes. Of course. He had this dog, you see—"

More laughter. *Pull yourself together. He's all serious and he'll think I'm crackers.*

"Fred, I'm sorry. I really want to hear your story, but, well, Calvin was born on the tenth of July."

"Who the hell is Calvin!"

"He was my husband's beloved dog in Jim's teen years. Born on the, well, on your date of birth. Although much later of course. And my husband wanted a really impressive name for his dog. So he had this idea that he would name him for someone famous born on the tenth of July. He went to the library and got a list of famous people and—"

"Stop at 'C,'" Fred said slowly. "Calvin."

"Yes." I smothered another burst of laughter. "John Calvin, the reformation fellow in Switzerland in the fifteen hundreds. I didn't know that until later. When we were first married Jim talked about Calvin a lot. 'My best friend,' he said. 'Taught me a lot about life.' 'Are you still in touch?' I asked him. 'No, he's gone,' he said, 'and a hard, hard day that was.'

"On the next tenth of July he told me who Calvin really was. His dog."

Fred gave me a long, serious look. Then he suddenly broke into a big grin.

"Your husband, he sounds like someone I would have enjoyed meeting."

I waved my hands. "Please. I'm so sorry. Go on with the story of your life."

He looked away. "Nancy and I had good moments like that in our marriage, too. We were close."

"Now I've distracted you. Please go on."

His eyes turned back to mine. "Very well."

"My father found work easily in the States and later, on Bohr's recommendation, he was involved in the Manhattan Project during World War Two.

"We lived in Forest Hills, Queens. I crossed boundaries and attended Brooklyn Poly. Got interested in electrical engineering. Went to MIT after, and a series of positions followed that led to involvement in the development of the integrated circuit and later on projects that have given us lucky people personal computers, laptops, cellphones, and, more recently, Google and Facebook, Twitter and Tweets.

"Along the way I married Nancy, a wonderful woman and a great mom for our two children. We had a large, comfortable house in Cos Cob, Connecticut, and we all learned to sail on a large, comfortable boat. Bored yet?"

"No, just feeling a bit overwhelmed."

"Scientists are like that. Remember, you're next."

"No, no. Please go on."

"Not much more. In her later years, my beautiful Nancy dealt with multiple sclerosis and died ten years ago, surrounded by everyone who loved her."

He paused and looked away.

"I know how that feels," I said softly.

Fred looked at me. His eyes were moist. "All my scientific know-how and there was nothing I could do."

"I understand the feeling. My Jim died of lung cancer."

He cocked his head at me. "So you do know."

"Yes."

"Life can seem pretty empty after that."

"Yes."

He cleared his throat. "So. I exchanged my boat for another one designed for solo sailing, and went sailing for three months. Down the Intra-Coastal to the Caribbean and across to Central America and back. When I returned I sold the boat, sold the house, split the net proceeds into two trusts at the lifetime gift limits for the college education of my five grandchildren with my son and daughter as trustees. I moved to a condo on Long Island Sound in Queens."

He gave me a level look. "Are you okay with this?"

I nodded, chin in hand.

"Well, I'll be honest. Did the bar scene. Answered personals. Nothing worked out. No magic moment. So in the end I found a co-op near Brooklyn Poly two years ago. I've taught some classes there to keep a hand in. Most of my time has been spent feeling sorry for myself."

"Have you no friends?"

"Yes, but when you're a long time married, wives seem to have the close friendships. I retired and realized most of my friendships had been in work relationships. When work stops men don't have much to talk about except gripes and groans. I see the guys occasionally but the conversation all revolves around closing the loop and—"

"Closing the loop?"

"Sorry. I was in therapy for a while. Closing the loop is what one does as the realization of mortality presses in. What has it all meant? One's life."

"I'd think you'd consider yourself quite successful."

"Sure. Career, money, lots of gizmos and *things*. Lots and lots of things."

He stopped.

"Blah blah blah. Your turn."

I told him about Jim and about our parents and about Steve and about the other two children who turned out differently than Jim and I had hoped. I told him about Jim's work at the Navy Yard until it finally closed after SeaTrain. I told him about The Russell House and the friends I had there. There was much more but I finally ended.

His eyes were on mine the whole time. At one point he put a hand on my hand and I let him keep it there.

As I spoke, he became a friend, no longer a stranger. From time to time he gave me a sympathetic glance or a smile that indicated, yes, he knew how that was. He kept his hand on mine, and the warmth was comforting in a very basic way.

Near the end of my part of our conversation, an image grew larger and larger in my mind.

It was of one of the magnets at the top of my refrigerator door.

Life is not measured by the number of breaths we take, but by the number of moments that take our breath away.

At last my breath ran out. I stopped. And breathed in, deeply.

"Wow," he said quietly, "you've had quite a life."

"So have you."

"Do you think that—" He stopped. "No, that's much too forward." He withdrew his hand.

He leaned forward. "How about another round of coffee and croissants next Tuesday?"

"Let me look." I retrieved my pocket diary from my purse and checked the date.

"Yes," I nodded. "I have something else, but I can switch it around."

"Good." He smiled. "Thank you for coming today. Lucy."

I smiled back. "Thank *you* for coming today. Fred."

He glanced at his watch. "Three fifteen. If we hang around much longer they have a good menu for dinner."

"No, no." I laughed.

His eyes turned serious.

"We've been pretty straight with each other, don't you agree?"

I nodded. I wondered where this comment would lead. He stood and beckoned to the woman who was still seated across the otherwise now empty room.

He turned back to me as the woman rose and walked toward us.

"Lucy, I want you to meet someone who is very special to me."

The woman stood next to him and smiled at me, a warm, generous smile. Side by side with Fred, her features were quite similar.

"Lucy, this is my daughter Elizabeth."

I was speechless. His daughter reached out a hand and I shook it.

"I am very glad to meet you," she said. "Dad has been going on and on about this wonderful woman he met at the library."

I looked at Fred. "But we knew nothing about each other."

Fred smiled. 'I told you what I saw."

I was nonplussed. "What does this mean?"

His daughter answered. "My father has been through some really tough times in recent years and I became concerned about the women he's been seeing. In fact, I meddled." She laughed. "I mean, what's a daughter to do when she's sure her father is sailing down the wrong river."

Fred grimaced. 'Lucy, please don't take offense."

"I've never heard of such a thing!"

Elizabeth gave me a shrewd glance. "I've been his minder long enough. From what I observed in your conversation, I don't think I need to worry any longer."

"Now, wait a minute, Liz," her father said. "No pressure, please. On me or on Lucy."

"Not to worry." She took my hand in hers. "I am so very glad to meet you. You have a wonderful laugh." She smiled, "You'll learn that he's not at all a dry stick. And now, I'm going back to my world in Manhattan. Bye."

I released her hand. She walked back to her table to pick up her purse and walk to the door. She opened it and turned for one last brilliant smile.

"Bye, Dad and Lucy. Have fun!"

Six months later Niels Frederik Jorgensen sold his co-op and moved into The Russell House. By then we were lovers.

15

AFTER HIS MOVE TO The Russell House, Fred announced that he wanted to accompany me to church on Sundays. I had placed no pressure on him and I was pleased that he voluntarily offered.

As we walked past the Widows' Club in the atrium of the church, I smiled as I felt the eyes of the group of women on me.

So much had changed since the meeting I attended. People "hooked up" electronically. Politicians sent sensuous photos. Be careful what you text; be careful what you say. The world may be watching and listening.

Pastor Roger had moved on to his next posting, as had Pastor Ted. So the Methodist procedure goes. After Ted, there was Pastor Roy, in whose pastorate the sanctuary was redone. New paint, stained glass windows cleaned, an audio system, ramps built in place of stairs to the sanctuary, and some pews removed at the back and the front to accommodate wheelchairs.

We were mostly an aging church except for a group of Brazilian Methodists who lived nearby in their own Brooklyn enclave. They were in their thirties and forties and had children; the younger children from time to time would break loose from a parental grasp and scamper away up the aisle to the back during the pastor's sermon.

The Brazilians were fairly well to do. The men worked for various Brazilian firms in New York and most spoke English. Once a month they held a Saturday evening dinner dance in Fellowship Hall. There were complaints from neighbors about loud music.

C.C. Hutchinson was still around. She had a motorized wheelchair and was rumored to hold races on the sidewalk outside the church with the Brazilian children. Life was good.

16

EARLY IN THE WEEK of my 85th birthday, my daughter Sophie called and said she wanted to see me about an important matter.

She arrived. We engaged in the usual pleasantries for a few minutes.

"How is Pru?" I asked.

"Busy working on canvases for a gallery show in Soho in December. It's a big step forward."

"How is Pru's daughter?"

"Maris is okay. Now in high school and hormones are hopping."

"I hope that's manageable."

"Well enough, it seems. Pru talks to her. I stay out of it."

More along this line. Sophie's eyes were blinking more rapidly than usual, a sign since her childhood of inner agitation.

"How is Fred?" she asked suddenly.

"He's fine. Thank you again for inviting us both over to dinner."

"I – we – were glad to meet him."

"Good."

Pause. My daughter glanced away.

"Sophie, you obviously want to talk to me about something."

She would not look at me.

"Yes. It's about Fred."

"And?"

She turned to face me, lips pursed.

"He seems like a very nice, intelligent man. I assume by now you are closer than just friends."

I did not respond.

She sighed. "I assumed as much."

"Why are you sighing? Why not be glad for me?"

"Well, Mother, it's just that it's been so long. I mean, all these years since Dad died. You've been like a nun in a convent. And then all of a sudden, Fred."

I spoke softly. "If we're lucky, maybe lightning strikes twice. First, your father, and now, Fred."

"But the suddenness of it all. I find in my own work with older women that aging can dull one's perception of reality."

"I have a pretty good handle on reality, thank you."

"I'm worried that you're rushing into things without exploring the consequences."

'Such as?"

She looked away and didn't answer.

"Sophie. You're my daughter. You don't need to treat me like a piece of fine china. Or one of the people that comes to you for counseling. What are you worried about?"

She addressed the far wall. "For one thing, I gather that he got around a bit since his wife died."

"He's told me that. So?"

"Well, there are diseases, STDs."

"Sophie, look at me, please."

She turned back to face me.

I looked at her. She genuinely was concerned for me. I kept my voice matter-of-fact.

"Before we first were intimate, Fred had a complete and thorough medical exam. His decision. Nothing showed up. In fact, he is in excellent physical condition for a man his age."

"That's a relief." She paused. "Did you see a copy of the report?"

"Yes. What else are you concerned about?"

"Financial stuff. Some of the women I counsel have told me terrible stories about being conned by nice, intelligent men."

"For heaven's sake, Sophie!"

"How much do you have in investments now?"

"It's really none of your business."

"Mother! Are you going to be destitute at some point? That's what my brother and I worry about. You'll be dependent on us."

"You don't need to worry. I have something over six hundred thousand in conservative investments. I don't touch it. I live on my pension and social security and am able to add some money most months to my portfolio. And I have group long term care insurance. In case."

"Has he asked for any money from you?"

"No."

"Special gifts?"

"No."

"Are you planning to marry?"

"Periodically he proposes, but at this stage of our relationship, I think that is an unwise move simply because we both have our own ways. Being too close might stifle our relationship."

"Are you thinking of merging households?"

"No. Same reason."

"If you do decide to marry, I hope you'll have a prenuptial agreement."

I'd had enough.

"Sophie, I appreciate your concern but I am *not* some woman who doesn't know how to size up a man or balance her checkbook or monitor her investments, investments which you and your brother will inherit."

"It's not about money for us. I just want you to enjoy life and be safe."

"Well, don't worry. You and Jim will get a pot from dear old Mom. And I *am* enjoying life."

"I do hope you'll think about the possibility of a pre-nup."

"Yes, yes. Now, unless you have something else to talk about, I think it's time to say 'good-bye.'"

After a few more comments, she left. Fortunately I had a three o'clock bridge date or I would have begun to think dark thoughts.

At home again later, I fixed a tomato and lettuce salad with a can of tuna poured on top, got a glass of Pinot Grigio and adjourned to the living room to watch the news at six.

Fred was on a business trip to California, checking on a firm that was using one of his personal patents to develop improved forms of prosthetic limbs. He called at seven New York time.

I was so glad to hear his voice! I didn't tell him about Sophie's visit. He sensed something though.

"Sweetie, are you okay? You sound a little subdued."

"I'm okay. Been a long day."

"Things have gone well and I'm wrapping it up over dinner with the folks here. If you like, I can catch the red-eye at midnight."

"No, no. You know you don't sleep well on planes. I'm okay. Really."

"All right. With the time change on my flight tomorrow, I'll be at JFK by four and at the house by six. Earlier if the traffic isn't too heavy."

"I'll be glad to see you. Take a shower and come down. I'll fix a light supper and you can tell me about your adventures."

"It's a deal, Lucile. See you tomorrow. Love you."

"Love you, too, Fred. So very much. I'm missing you."

In the end he took the red-eye and knocked on my door at ten a.m.

I was so glad to see him! During the night my spirit had tumbled into the past and I reverted to heavy Worry Mode.

We looked at each other after I opened the door.

Simultaneously we said, "You don't look like you got much sleep!"

We both laughed as he swung his suitcase into the living room and walked in.

"I started worrying about you, so I came on. What's up?"

"My daughter came by and expressed her concerns about you and me."

He gave me a hug and we stayed close. "Sounds serious."

"Things are always serious with Sophie. Now the spotlight is on Dear Old Mom."

"C'mon. Let's sit down and talk."

"Oh, Fred, not now. We're both tired. You go upstairs and take a nap and have a shower and then come down."

He held me away from him and looked at me. "Promise you'll take a nap, too."

"Promise." I kissed him. "I'm so glad you're home. If you have things to wash, leave your suitcase here."

"Okay."

The summit meeting convened at noon with grilled cheese sandwiches and tomato bisque soup.

"All right," he said when we had finished. "What did your daughter say that upset you?"

He reached over and took my right hand in his.

"I'll tell you as succinctly as I can."

"We have the rest of the day. Don't rush."

"I'm going to tell you what she said but I want you to promise me you'll stay calm."

"Certainly."

"You've met her and her partner. That may not have been enough for you to form an idea about Sophie."

"I enjoyed meeting them. They appear to be a good match. Your daughter did seem a bit hyper."

"She usually is."

"Dear Lucy. Tell me."

I told him. Practically word for word of our twenty-minute conversation in the living room.

Fred's eyes changed to a twinkle as I recounted the disease bit. He started grinning when I got to the 'con man' bit. He let go of my hand and began laughing before I reached the end.

He wiped the tears from his eyes. "Oh my, my, my. You must have been ready to blow your top!"

"She means well," I said, "but her concern is misplaced."

"She has a point. I haven't explicitly spoken of my financial situation."

"You have told me there is more than enough for us. If it comes to that."

"Oh, Lucy. Always this hesitation. Marry me."

"I don't want to ruin our relationship."

"What's to ruin? We go out together. We watch TV together most evenings. I have sleepovers with you several nights a week. We attend church together. How will marriage be different?"

"I can't explain it except to say again, you have a place, I have a place. It's the best way."

"Lucy, I have two words in response: grumble, grumble."

He smiled.

"Okay, let's talk about finances. I'll bring down a copy of my last tax return, but it's thirty-five pages long."

"You know what I have."

"Yes. And that's good. Always more income than outgo. Me, too."

"Fred, I don't want your children to get less because of our relationship, married or not. That's very important to me."

"You've said as much several times before. I thank you. My daughter and my son thank you.

"Not to worry. When I sold the house in Connecticut, and the boat, I took the hit in taxes despite the counsel of my CPA and split the remainder between them for college education of their kids. I simply didn't want that issue to hang over me. I have considerable investments in a diversified portfolio with one of the no-load fund companies. I have made my son and daughter beneficiaries. When I go, it's theirs."

He yawned and stretched his arms.

"In addition I have a sizable pension, social security, which is wiped out by my taxes, and semi-annual royalty payments from a dozen or so of my patents that are in active use."

"You certainly can afford to live in a place more posh than The Russell House."

"Goofus, I want to be near you. This has been your home and you want to stay here. Okay, then that's where I want to be."

"Oh, Fred." I reached out and caressed his face. "My life would be so empty without you."

He clasped my hand. "Likewise, dear one."

"Now," he continued, "if you want to arrange a meeting between me and your children, I will be glad to assure them that I am not a—what was the word?"

"Con man."

"Or you can tell them to look me up on the internet. My bio is quite a puff piece. Should reassure them."

"It's really none of their business."

"But they need to be reassured I won't hijack your assets and leave you dependent on them. That's the big scare."

"I suppose." I stifled a yawn. "Sorry, not enough sleep last night."

Fred yawned. "Me, too. My nap wasn't long enough." He smiled. "Any chance—"

"Yes, I think we should go and have a nice lie-down together. But you have to be good and really nap."

"I will. Sooner or later."

17

"Two juice boxes," announced Tony.

We were at my kitchen table, extenders in, filling grocery bags with supplemental weekend food for eleven children in Tony and Benjy's class. Every item was handed around to the nine of us at the table. Tony and Benjy each filled a bag at the end.

"Peanut butter crackers," Tony called out.

It was another Thursday evening's activity for The Russell House Eleven.

I had indeed spoken to Mrs. Logan. For six weeks now we had assembled on Thursday in my apartment to unload the cartons of food that Carlos had picked up during the week.

Daisy furnished extra folding chairs.

"Raisins," Tony said.

"Ramen noodles."

It was Thursday evening two weeks after Jim Junior had left. I had not heard from him while he was in London, and that was just as well. I was not budging from my position.

"Tuna."

Mrs. Logan had told me that brown grocery bags were preferable to separate backpacks. Most students who received them managed to stuff them in their own backpacks.

"Oatmeal."

The two boys, Carlos, Rosa, Mr. K, Fred, Angie, Daisy, Abe, Rebecca, and I all had made a commitment to meet every Thursday evening at seven o'clock. Carlos brought the cartons of food items from three different groceries.

"Applesauce."

Rebecca amazed us all. For her it was a definite set task, and she filled up her grocery bag just as we all did.

"Breakfast Bar."

Filling the bags took about thirty minutes. At the end of packing, I wheeled my large grocery cart over to the table and we placed the bags in it. I delivered them to the school principal every Friday morning at ten.

We were finishing up as there was a knock at the door. Abe pushed back his chair.

"I'll get it," he said. "Special guest."

He opened the door and stepped back as an attractive woman in her sixties entered. Daisy eyed her and snorted.

"Daisy," I cautioned.

"Everyone," said Abe, "I'd like you to meet my cousin Beatrice."

"Cousin!" Daisy half rose in her chair.

"Yes, she's been here in 1 C," he looked at his cousin, "how long is it?"

"Six weeks."

"That's right. And Beatrice —"

"Oh, Abe, so formal!" She gave us all a smile. "Please call me Bea."

She looked at the grocery cart that Carlos and Mr. K were placing the last bags into.

"My goodness. What's all this."

Mr. K straightened up.

"Supplemental food packs for second-graders at our local school. For the weekend. On weekdays the children receive two good meals a day. But for many of the youngsters, as a general rule, weekend meals in their homes are meager or non-existent. For them, these food packs are given out at the end of school on Friday to take home. It's our way of building a neighborhood that cares for its kids."

Bea stepped to the grocery cart and Carlos opened the bag on top.

"My goodness, that's a lot of food," she exclaimed.

Daisy spoke up. "I've seen your face in the newspapers!"

Bea ignored her. "This is a wonderful thing you are doing!"

Abe gave Daisy a look and said to us all, "What you need to know about Bea is—"

Bea gave him a wave of her hand.

"Please, Abe. I just want to meet my neighbors. May I sit down?"

Mr. K stood and pulled his chair out. "This one's available."

He joined Benjy and Tony, who were leaning against the kitchen counter.

"Thank you." Bea sat. She looked at Daisy.

"Yes, I have been in the newspapers from time to time. But those days are over."

She smiled at Mr. K and the two boys and then glanced around the table.

"I'm a newcomer here. I wanted a nice apartment in The Russell House and I'm fortunate one became available."

She placed her hands on the table. A simple gold ring was on one finger.

"I want to get to know my neighbors. I've met some. My cousin Abe told me about your Thursday evenings and invited me up. He has told me quite a bit about you. I'm Bea; now please tell me your names."

We introduced ourselves.

After we concluded she smiled again.

"I am very glad to meet you. Abe says you are the movers and shakers at The Russell House. Let me see if I have the basics about you that he's related to me."

She nodded to Benjy and Tony. "Benjy and Tony are in the second grade. They live on the sixth floor and are buddies through thick and thin. Benjy's father is Carlos, his mother is Rosa, and Tony's mother is Angie."

"My dad is an officer on the Queen Mary," volunteered Tony.

"Good for him!" Bea exclaimed.

Her gaze moved to Mr. K.

"Mr. K—what an interesting name! I hope I will learn what the 'K' stands for. You're on track for a pharmacy degree. At present you are a pharmacy assistant. You also are a mentor to four middle-school boys as a Big Brother volunteer. Impressive."

As she proceeded she nodded to each of us in turn.

"Carlos got caught in a downsizing at his bank. He does odd jobs between interviews. Rosa has a position at Bloomingdale's.

"As Tony proudly told us, his father is an officer on the Queen Mary. Angie is a stay-at-home mom. In addition she cares for her mother-in-law."

She turned to me. "Mrs. Scott—may I call you Lucy?"

I nodded.

"Lucy is the venerable member of the group and recently celebrated her eighty-fifth birthday. Congratulations! Unfortunately she is presently at odds with her son and daughter."

I nodded vigorously. "They think I'm in a decline. They want to park me in a nursing home so they won't have to feel responsible. They think I have no friends to help me. But here they are, and there are many more."

"You truly are blessed," smiled Bea. "May you be blessed with many more good years."

"Thank you."

She looked at Fred and her smile widened.

"Fred possesses a multitude of talents. What matters to him most, though, is his love for Lucy. He wants to marry her so they can help each other in the years ahead."

Fred exclaimed, "You got that right!"

Bea turned to Daisy and her smile faded.

"Daisy, ah Daisy. A fixture years ago in Broadway song and dance. Is that correct?"

"Yes. Good times long ago. Never top of the bill, but only two steps away!"

Bea's voice softened. "I understand that you have experienced great tragedy in your life. It is wonderful that you have a support group here."

She looked around the table. "Have I touched on a bit of your lives?"

We all nodded except for Abe and Rebecca. I discreetly pointed my finger in their direction just as Rebecca began to sing.

"When I am gone —who will remember
what I was in my prime.

The old ways, the golden days,
The way I used to be."
Abe patted her on the shoulder. "Not now, dear."
"And finally," Bea continued, "my cousin Abraham. Loyal to his wife of forty years. The dear Rebecca. Loyal to the end. He needs some respite care. The burden is a heavy one to bear. He needs time out!"

Abe nodded to her. "Thank you, Bea, so very nicely done. Speaking of time—"

She waved him off again and turned to the rest of us.

"And I want *you* to get to know *me*. Let me see now," she thought for a moment. "I grew up in New Jersey. My father was a Rabbi, so I always had to be prim and proper. But my father also loved mathematics and he encouraged me in that direction. So I took all the math courses I possibly could. By the time I graduated from Rutgers, I was ready for success."

She smiled. "We all have had obstacles to overcome. Mine was to be a company financial officer *and* a woman! It was quite something to go to conferences and to be the only woman there.

"I kept my head down and my mouth shut as I endured a ton of patronizing talk around me as I moved up from office to office. It paid off big time!

"I became a financial wizard on the corporate trail, cleaning up companies whose executives were just plain stupid or they couldn't keep pace with their company's growth. In a couple of cases the guys at the top were milking the assets – and they went to jail for it. I loved those companies! There I was sitting at a long table with corporate directors who were quaking in their boots, not knowing what to do financially and afraid the SEC would be looking at them next!

"Investment companies and shareholders made me a celebrity and I had a new name: 'Bea, the Fix-It Queen.'

"At forty-three I married Harry. We were quite a corporate pair! He had an incredible talent for sniffing out commercial properties in areas that were about to rebound in New York City. His

Rolodex was a doorway to the city's Who's Who. He knew who to kowtow to and who to screw."

Gasps around the table.

"Pardon the language, but that's the way we worked. I was the financial wizard. He was the real estate whiz. Me and Harry – the Real Estate Baron and the Fix-It Queen. And after every success, he'd say, 'The tigers score again! I'll always love you, Bea, till the day I die.'" She sighed. "And he did. Till the day he died."

She paused and looked around at us, one by one. "I know I'm going on and on, but I've never said all this to anybody else. You and I — we're going to be like family, I hope. And what I've learned is that every family has a heart ache. Me, too."

"What happened?" Carlos asked.

"Harry died when I was sixty-one. I never imagined such a thing. I had this crazy notion that we'd go on together from success to success."

We all were hushed, one question in every mind: why on earth was the Fix-It Queen living at The Russell House?

"And the hardest thing was to keep going with the charities we helped. We had a suite at the Pierre on Fifth Avenue. I came back from the funeral and there were stacks of invitations on my desk, awaiting my personal note. 'Help the Public Library.' 'Save the City Opera.' 'Keep Sesame Street going.' Gala Balls. Magnificent Dinners. Fundraiser after fundraiser. I was at the head of a charity machine."

"I knew it," shrieked Daisy. She rose from her chair and held her arms up as though scoring a touchdown. "That's it! The society pages. I knew I'd seen your picture!"

"Oh, the noise, the noise," complained Rebecca. Daisy sat.

"Yes, there were many pictures. But none lately. Because one day—"

She paused, her eyes moist.

"Late one morning, after yet another night at a gala for one worthy cause or another . . . I looked in the mirror and did not recognize the person looking back at me. A woman with a face so worn and lined that no amount of makeup or spa treatments could repair. And I suddenly thought of the rush of emotion I felt on the day I walked off the commencement stage at Rutgers, diploma in hand. I was free! And now, I hungered for that feeling – to be free again!"

She paused again. "Are there any tissues handy?"

"Benjy, by the sink," I said. He passed the box of tissues over and Carlos placed it in front of Bea.

She took one and blew her nose. "Thank you," she said, and gave a little laugh. "I must seem like a tired old woman to you."

Murmurs of "no, no, not at all," from around the table.

"You're sure to be wondering why I am sitting here this evening, a resident of The Russell House. I would be wondering if I were in your place."

Abe reached a hand over and patted her on the shoulder.

"Take your time," he said.

"What I did next may seem incredible to you, but I did it. Sold the companies, gave away the jewelry, ditched the après ski parties in Davos, threw off the public relations firm, told all the charities that I was through."

"Yes," Fred murmured, smiling. "Oh, yes."

"I wanted to get out of the Pierre, out of Manhattan, to a place I could be free. I've found it. The Russell House, apartment 1 C."

She took another tissue and blew her nose again. When she continued, her voice was stronger.

"So, I guess the moral of the mirror is about the meaning of fame. You can win a fortune for yourself and still be losing the game."

She smiled at us. "Now I'm a very different Fix-It Queen, humbler and more aware of helping people who need help. I have established a foundation to develop new kinds of affordable housing for people in Africa and Asia and in the USA. And you can find the new and improved me, happy and satisfied, living downstairs in Apartment 1 C."

Silence as we all digested the Story of Bea. At last Fred spoke.

"Yours is a story of great courage. I'm still back there wondering why you chose The Russell House. There are other more modern apartment houses in Brooklyn that are adjacent to one of the parks. Why here?"

"Yes, Fred. There *are* any number of places I could have chosen. Or in Queens, the Bronx, even Staten Island."

She stopped, her eyes downcast.

"This particular building," she went on, "has a special meaning for me. My husband grew up in 1 C. Moving here is a way of keeping faith with him." She smiled. "Nothing spooky and I'm not planning séances. Just a feeling that he's near."

More sympathetic murmurings around the table.

There was a firm knock at the door. I rose from the table and went to open it. Jim Junior was standing there with his briefcase. He gave me a level look.

"Hi, Mom. I'm back."

"I was expecting a call."

"Other things are going on."

"Oh."

"I'm on my way to a Long Island evening meeting. Figured I'd stop off on the way and say hello."

"Hello."

"Have you made a choice?"

"No."

"Look, do you mind if I come in."

I opened the door wider and he passed by me.

"Oh, you have company."

"These are my friends."

"Look, I don't have a lot of time." He addressed the group around the table and the three leaning against the counter. "Excuse us, please."

He turned to me. "Let's go into the living room."

He had his hand on my arm and was pulling me toward the other room. I planted my feet.

"No."

"Mom, tomorrow's the deadline. Have you decided?"

"I'm staying here."

He smiled and spoke to me patiently, as if I were a child instead of his mother.

"Two weeks ago, remember, Mom? We talked about it and you were going to make a decision."

"You made a decision. Not me."

His voice rose. "Now don't go all stubborn on me."

He looked at the others, staring at my family drama.

"Mom, let's go in the other room."

I pulled my arm away.

"No. I want to live here. This is my home. Not some place in New Jersey or out on Long Island."

He put his briefcase down. "These are three good places you can afford."

"Wonderful. Cooped up with a group of old people waiting to die. I want to live. Here."

He sighed. "Mom, it's the help you need."

"No. This is what I need. Look around. These are my friends."

He sighed and addressed the others.

"I'm sorry to involve you all in this. But I can't wait any longer. My mother has had a good life but now she's at a stage where she needs some help. I am grateful for your friendship, but she has to make a choice about what comes next."

"I'm staying here."

"Mother, don't be stubborn now. I have to put your name in by tomorrow noon. Which place is it gonna be?"

I glared at him. The silence was broken by Bea, speaking in a very cultured voice.

"Why, Mr. Scott! So good to see you again. I had no idea that Lucy is your mother."

She stood, smiling, as Jim Junior stared, trying to place her.

"Let me think," Bea continued. "Oh, yes. MOMA, the Museum of Modern Art, a year ago February. You and your lovely wife sat at Table Eight with other special guests."

My son was beginning to boil.

"Look, lady, whoever you are. I've got business with my mother that we need to get on with. So excuse me." His head turned back to me. "Well?"

"I just—I just—"

"You stubborn old woman! All right, time's up. I figured as much so I've already made the choice. Long Island. That's where I'm headed now, to sign the contract. Movers are coming in Monday at one to pack up."

Carlos had had enough. I saw him rise, angry.

"What gives you the right to talk to your Mama like that!"

"Carlos." Mr. K moved over from the kitchen counter and put a hand on Carlos' shoulder. Carlos shook it off.

My son looked at him scornfully. "Who are you? The janitor?"

With a roar Carlos lunged forward, fists up. My son lashed out with his right fist and punched him hard on the jaw. Carlos, lip bleeding, fell back on Mr. K, who grabbed both his arms and held him. Carlos struggled to get loose.

"You son of a bitch!"

Mr. K held him tighter. "Carlos, no! He'll come down on you like a ton of bricks!"

He pulled Carlos backward to the counter as Tony and Benjy looked on wide-eyed.

My son dusted off the lapels of his expensive suit and remarked in a silky tone: "Your friend is correct. Tsk, tsk. All these witnesses. Well, let me show you all what I was about to show my mother."

He lifted his briefcase from the floor, walked to the table and placed the briefcase in front of where Bea had sat. He opened the briefcase and took out several sheets of paper.

"I knew she wouldn't do anything while I was away on a business trip. So . . . I had some of my people do the legwork for me."

He held up a number of papers in succession, returning each to the briefcase as he spoke.

"One. This is a complaint to the Management Company from Dominica Cartage. Seems they haven't been paid for replacing the dumpster twice a month, so they are stopping service. Dated one month ago.

"Two. Copies of letters from residents here to the Management Company, complaining about your resident super's bouts of drinking. Days on end, it seems. Quite a rude fellow.

"Three: Copies of letters to the city commission on housing. Complaints by residents about lack of exterminator services and no answer when they call the Management Company's phone.

"Four: Court papers filed for bankruptcy by the Management Company one month ago, stating that the company has a negative asset balance of one million eight hundred fifty thousand dollars and they cannot continue operations.

"Five: A proposal to the Brooklyn Land and Property Commission by a construction company to purchase The Russell House, not a listed historic property, demolish it, and build a twenty-story luxury condo apartment house in its place."

He paused and smiled as he returned the last sheet to his briefcase and closed and latched it.

"My sources tell me they expect approval within two months."

He looked around at the group. "Just seven weeks from today."

He put both hands on the closed briefcase and glanced at the two boys, Carlos and Mr. K and around at the rest.

"I understand you are friends in Mom's circle. I appreciate that and I thank you. But she's leaving this dump next week. I advise all of you to start looking for other housing. The demolition should begin around the first week in March."

Carlos spat out, "And a Merry Christmas to you, too!"

Jim Junior turned to him. "Face facts, sonny. Can't stop progress."

He looked at me. "'Bye, Mom." Pointed a forefinger at me. "Moving van will be here at one on Monday."

He picked up his briefcase and exited. For once he closed the door quietly behind him.

In the stunned silence that followed we all listened to the sound of the elevator taking him to the first floor.

Bea and I sat down. On one side of me Angie put her arm around my shoulder. On the other side, Fred took my hand.

Mr. K released Carlos. Carlos came back to the table and sat, muttering.

"Man oh man oh man."

At last Bea spoke.

"Something tells me he won't be asking for an apartment here."

Nervous laughter from around the table.

Benjy and Tony crossed over from the kitchen counter and stood by my side. Tony put his hand on top of his mother's arm that was hugging me. Benjy patted me on my other shoulder and looked at Fred. Fred shook his head.

I broke the silence, speaking slowly.

"I am so ashamed you all had to witness that. Carlos, are you okay?"

"Yeah, yeah, I'm all right." He turned to Mr. K. "Thanks."

I sighed. "I just don't understand. He was a lovely child. Now, every time he comes around, my bones feel old and cold."

Daisy slapped her hands on the table, pushed her chair back and stood.

"We need a lift. We gotta get moving so we can shake it off!"

Rebecca angrily waved her hand. "No, no, no, no," she shouted. "Sit down!"

Squelched, Daisy sat.

"Wherever you go, honey" said Fred firmly, "I'll be there."

It was all so stupid, stupid, stupid.

"I don't want to be *there*, I belong *here*! Monday at one, huh! They'll have to carry me out!"

Abe looked at me and spoke. "Bea, tell them."

"Tell us what?" Carlos asked.

Bea sighed and sat up straight in her chair. "What I have to say won't change Lucy's situation with her son. However, it may relieve your minds about the bogeyman of imminent demolition and we all have to move."

We waited while she thought of how to say what she wanted to tell us.

"All right, here it is. What happens between James Scott, Junior and his mother is between them."

A visceral growl from Mr. K.

"I know, I know." Bea continued. "But the threat of what he told us has no solid foundation."

"I think I know what's coming." Daisy smiled.

Bea smiled at her. "I said I sold all the companies. I kept one. The one that has the contract with the now-bankrupt management company." She paused.

"The fact is, I own the building."

The room resounded with exclamations and laughter.

Rebecca, puzzled, asked, "Did I miss a joke?"

Bea turned to her. "It's not a joke Rebecca. It's about the latest chapter in my life. I wanted a new place to live that would mean something to me. I inquired, and Apartment 1 C was available."

"Quite a change for you!" exclaimed Daisy.

"Yes. But as I told you, 1 C has a special meaning for me. It's where my husband lived as a child until he went away to the university."

Mr. K looked puzzled. "Hold on. Didn't you call your husband the real estate baron?"

"He was. His father built this apartment house and dozens of others. Park Slope, the Heights, all over. The others were sold, but he kept this one. My husband inherited it. He went on to buy and build bigger buildings, but he kept this one for sentimental reasons. I inherited it from him. I heard that there were problems developing here, so I came to find out for myself."

Daisy was triumphant. "You're Mrs. Russell! *The* Mrs. Russell."

"Just plain Bea in 1 C now. I wanted to find out what the tenants are like. I wanted to discover whether any real community existed here or if people were impersonal and it was time to let it go.

"My cousin Abe," a smile at him, "did his best to persuade me there indeed is a strong community, but I still wasn't sure. And then this issue about Lucy came up and I was sure. You've come together for Lucy, and that is a wonderful thing."

Mr. K slapped the tabletop.

"Right! What men like her son can't take is public embarrass-ment. So he's having the moving van people come on Monday. Let's think of how to prevent them from getting to Lucy."

"Turn off the elevator?" suggested Benjy.

"Good idea, but I don't think so. They could take three flights of stairs."

Tony spoke. "They can't get in the front door without a key, and if nobody answers the buzzer?"

I sighed. "They'll have the key I gave my son. I'm sure he'll come, too."

Silence. Mental wheels were whirring.

Mr. K snapped his fingers.

"Right. What we need to do is up the stakes. Get others in-volved. We'll stand out front, blocking the door. Don't let the mov-ers or Junior in, you with me? He'll call in the cops. We'll call all the TV stations. The cops start hauling us away, and it'll be the lead clip on the evening local news. 'Hard-hearted son wants to force 85-year-old mother from her home of—' he turned to me—"how many years you been here?"

"Over fifty."

"Let's say, sixty. Just think. TV cameras, people from the Com-mission on Aging, folks from the AARP. Wooooeee!"

Daisy gave him a sour look.

"Wonderful! Face it—nobody gives a damn about us old farts. So she gets shoved out. So what!"

"But it's not right," protested Rosa. The others nodded.

Rebecca chimed in. "This is serious!"

Carlos shook his head. "My Mama said, there's always a way."

"Yes," agreed Fred. "There must be a way. But we've got to do it together. This is the time and this is the place. We need to do it here. We need to save Lucy from moving. Now."

""I've got it." Mr. K smiled. He looked around the table. "Any-body remember what Monday is."

"November 11th. Veterans Day," I replied. "I always remember."

"Right. Public school holiday. Lot of firms close. Means people may be available."

Fred smiled. "I think I see where you're going with this."

"Yes." Mr. K looked at Benjy and Tony. "Think you could get a dozen or so of your friends from school to show up."

"Sure!"

"People from our building, too," agreed Abe.

"I get the day off," Rosa said. "Could be the case with others."

Fred got excited. "Right! But we need organization." He looked around the table. "Right here, between us, we've got three out of six floors covered. Knock on doors today. We can split the other three. We're calling a meeting of all residents in the lobby at 10 am Saturday."

"And Saturday," added Carlos, "Mr. K gives the pitch and Fred calls for everybody to help out. This isn't just one 85-year-old. We're *all* affected. Old folks, young folks –everybody."

Daisy was enthusiastic. "We need chants and cheers! We need banners and posters! Maybe a conga line! I'll be in charge of all that."

"We have the beginning of a plan for Monday," said Abe, "but what's protecting Lucy till then?"

Fred smiled. "I am."

Bea turned to me. "Lucy, for your safety, you have to do two things."

"Anything!"

"I'm going to call a locksmith *now*. You want your apartment door locks changed by noon tomorrow if not sooner. Junior really will have to call you in advance from now on. Second, does your son hold your medical power of attorney?"

"Yes. Unfortunately."

"As soon as the doctor's office opens tomorrow morning, you'll call and revoke it. He's still your son but you'll have an edge. If it needs to be done in person, we'll go together."

The food pack meeting ended with assignments about who was to do what.

They left. I played all my favorite Edith Piaf songs over and over on my stereo until ten.

I slept well.

18

MONDAY DAWNED WITH LOVELY sunshine. On Sunday Fred had left to work out organizational details. I had a simple supper and slept soundly.

Daisy showed up at eight to begin transferring downstairs to the lobby the fifty picket signs stashed in my kitchen. There were six basic messages:

NO MOVE, NO WAY! RUSSELL HOUSE UNITED! HANDS OFF LUCY! REMOVE THE MOVE! BROOKLYN IS BEST! and my favorite, *85 AND STILL KICKIN'.*

Angie arrived shortly after and took the furled thirty-foot long banner up to the sixth floor to hang from the apartment windows facing the park. The banner was white canvas with yard-high painted lettering that declared, *"I'VE STLL GOT A LOT OF LIVING TO DO!" LUCY.*

Mrs. Logan had done the lettering for the signs and banner with the help of her two sons and their high school friends.

Fred went up to Daisy's apartment and brought down folding chairs for the dozen persons who had signed up to guard my door beginning at eleven. Fred was in charge of the 'house guard.' Other residents had donated thirty more folding chairs for use in the lobby by the group that was to do a sit-in there, starting at noon.

Two hot dog vendors were scheduled to show up by eleven thirty. Dear Fred had agreed to pay all their expenses until three.

The basic plan for the outside was to fill the sidewalk to the entrance with rotations of people who would alternate standing and then sitting on the planter benches along the side of the front walk. The sidewalk by the street would have two conga lines of girls from a dance school run by a friend of Daisy. The girls were bringing pom-poms. Mrs. Logan's sons had enlisted the aid of members of the high school marching band to play music.

Abe was bringing flyers that described the basic situation. He'd run them off on his former firm's photocopy machine.

Carlos was Grand Master of the outdoors. Mr. K was Spokesperson if one were needed. Bea was confident we would. She had made contact with the newspapers, TV and radio stations.

At noon I served sandwiches and soft drinks to the guardians outside my door. Fred stood by the elevator doors, cell phone in hand.

A long silence.

I walked over to Fred and gave him a hug.

"Dear Fred," I whispered, "what if nothing happens? What if my son changed his mind and it's tomorrow the movers are coming?"

Fred gave me a big smile. "Won't happen. This is 'showdown' time for Junior. Today."

Just then we heard a piercing whistle from the street below and the band began playing.

Fred's cellphone rang. He listened. "Okay," he said and hung up.

"The moving van has arrived, followed by a black limousine."

His announcement was greeted with cheers by my guardians.

Fred looked at me. "Inside." He gave me a hug. "Lock the doors. I'll give a holler if anyone's trying to move through us out here. If the coast is clear you can give us periodic reports from your window perch."

I went.

Looking down from my third-floor kitchen window, the scene below was a colorful mosaic of moving bodies and waving picket signs, all swaying to the music of a football pep song played by the band.

The two conga lines began moving toward each other along the curb. One line wore blue outfits and the other red, both teams waving white pom-poms, They passed and turned to repeat.

My next-door neighbor was busily filling balloons from a helium tank. Another neighbor was attaching strings and handing the balloons out to youngsters.

The vendors already were doing a brisk business at opposite ends of the street.

Two men descended from the cab of the moving van. One of them surveyed the scene and turned toward the limousine, hands up in a 'what now?' gesture. The limousine driver got out and walked toward him. They conferred.

The limousine driver returned to the car. He leaned against the driver's side. A rear window rolled down. The driver gestured toward the crowd. Words were exchanged. He nodded, opened the rear door and Jim Scott, Junior emerged.

He paused for a moment to look up at my window. A long look. Then he lowered his head and walked toward the conga lines.

A CBS TV mobile remote van rolled up the street and parked behind the limousine. Several other cars and trucks drove up and parked, filling up space to the end of the block. People from neighboring buildings were coming out to see what was happening.

I looked back down at the scene. The crowd below was still in motion. Passing through it Mr. K had walked over to where my son stood at the curb. They spoke.

The conference was a brief one. Mr. K turned away. My son looked up at me in my window and shook his head. He turned and walked to the moving van. He and the driver exchanged thoughts. He walked back to the limousine and the driver opened the door for him.

The TV van transmitter disc was at full height as the limousine drove off. One of the moving van men walked down the street to a vendor and shortly came back with a large sack. He and the driver got in the van. I hoped they would leave also, but the van sat motionless as they ate their free lunch.

The telephone in my living room rang and I hurried to answer. It was Fred.

"Bea just came up. She wants to come in."

"Okay."

I unlocked the door and a beaming Bea rushed in.

"Oh, Lucy," she exclaimed. "I really think I have surpassed myself! Have you seen any of the action?"

I pulled her through to my window perch. "I saw my son come—"

She interrupted me. "Look, look! They're going to do something."

We peered down. A young woman had gotten out of the passenger side of the van and was waiting by the hood. A man emerged from the back of the van and hoisted a mini-cam onto his shoulder. He walked to the front of the van. He and the woman had a long conversation.

At last the young woman nodded and they started across the street, reaching Mr. K, who had been joined by Carlos. The woman spoke to them both. At last there were nods all around. Carlos stepped away as the cameraman positioned himself in the middle of the street, looking for the best angle on the woman, the crowd and the building.

Bea's cell phone chirped.

"Yes? Really! That's great!"

She hung up. "Lucy, turn your living room TV on to CBS. They're doing an interview with Mr. K, a live feed to the midday news! I'll tell the others."

She raced to the door to tell the group in the hallway. I was just behind her to pick up the remote and turn on the television. My hands were shaking.

The hallway crew poured through the door, talking excitedly.

The television blinked on. The woman was standing in the street in front of the moving conga lines and beyond them a crowd of people in front of The Russell House. Blonde hair blowing in the breeze, she began to speak.

"John, it's an incredible scene on Veterans' Day. The building you see behind me is The Russell House, an older apartment house on the park in Brooklyn.

"There are several veterans here in uniform, but this gathering is in support of one woman, Lucy Scott. She's been a resident here for over 60 years and recently celebrated her eighty-fifth birthday. Mr. Kay, a resident, is ready to explain this phenomenal gathering."

Mr. K stepped into position beside her.

"Mr. Kay, what's going on here?" she asked.

"Linda, we're here to preserve the dignity of Lucy Scott. Her son thinks she needs to go to a nursing home, but we know better. We want her to stay on as a resident here."

"This is some crowd. Do all these people live in The Russell House?"

Behind them the Lucy signs were waving, among them ones that read, *Equal Rights for Seniors — AARP.*

"Many of them, Linda. Others come from the neighborhood, the elementary school, the high school. This is support from the whole community."

Two NYPD cars slowly drove up at one end of the street and stopped.

"Mr. Kay, what is so special about Lucy Scott? Look at all these people."

"We want her to have her rights observed. The moving van has come to take her things away. This is happening against her will."

"Have you spoken to her son – tried to work something out?"

"Her son made his position perfectly clear to a group of us last Thursday evening, Linda. He wants her to be properly cared for in an institution. But we all know she's perfectly capable of taking care of herself here. No need to move her elsewhere."

"Thank you for speaking to us. Hope you're successful."

The interviewer turned to face the camera.

"That's it, John. A mass rally in support of an elderly woman who wants to stay in her home. Mom versus son. And it's another kind of story for Veterans' Day. Mrs. Scott's other son, an Army officer, died while fighting in Iraq. Freedom is a cherished American value. Back to you."

An image of an older man filled the screen.

"Thanks, Linda. Interesting. A son who died in Iraq and another son who wants to move her against her will. A family conflict in Brooklyn on this Veterans' Day 2013. Hope it can be resolved. We'll be back with more local news after this commercial break."

My telephone rang. Carlos, his voice filled with excitement.

"Did you see it?"

"Sure did."

"What a day! This is fantastic!"

His tone changed.

"Are you at the kitchen window?"

"No. In the living room."

"Get to the kitchen window. Another news crew just arrived and a fellow is walking over to Mr. K and me." He hung up.

My guardians were talking loudly and slapping each other on the back as they returned to the hallway.

Fred moved against the tide and disappeared through the door to the kitchen. When he reappeared, his face was grim.

"Damn moving van is still there. We'll stay out here as long as it takes."

He closed the hallway door behind him.

Bea called to me, "Lucy, Carlos called. Fox News is here. Come look."

Fox News indeed was on the scene. So was the moving van, driver and partner still enjoying lunch in the cab. No one had emerged from the two police cars.

Bea's phone chirped.

"Yes."

A pause.

"I think she can do it. Send them up."

She hung up and looked at me.

"Fox News wants to interview you, Lucy. Are you okay with this?"

I thought.

"Yes."

We both peered down at the street. The conga lines were moving again and the pep band played. A cameraman was slowly panning across the crowd, the conga line, and the band.

"Lucy."

I looked at Bea.

"Do you have a nice, light-colored blouse? Perhaps blue, to bring out your eyes."

"Yes."

"Go put it on. Brush your hair. And think about what you wish to say. Firm but kind. Your son means well."

"All right."

I went to my bedroom and checked the contents of the closet. Yes, a lovely light blue blouse. I laid it on my bed while I brushed my hair to perfection.

I returned to the kitchen just as Bea's phone chirped again. "Hello?"

She held the cell phone out to me. "Fred." I took it.

"Lucy, darling. Carlos just called to say a crew from Fox News is coming up. Are you okay?"

"I think so."

"Just remember. Valedictorian and Phi Beta Kappa. Look straight into the camera and speak your piece. But don't whistle."

I felt my tension dissipate. I smiled. "Yes."

"I love you, Lucy."

"Love you, too."

He hung up. I handed the phone back to Bea. She was appraising me.

"You look great! I had a thought. Do you have a large photo of your son Steve?"

"In his room."

"Go get it," she directed, just as the doorbell chimed.

I retrieved the picture. It was a nicely framed photo of Steve, taken when he was promoted to Lieutenant Colonel.

When I returned to the kitchen, four people were crowded in with their equipment. One was adjusting lights on several stands. Another had a digital tape recorder that he had placed on the table and was fiddling with dials. The cameraman, video-cam on shoulder, was eyeing my family photo, and, next to it, the birthday card from Benjy.

"Huh." He turned and started to say something to the fourth man, who evidently was not involved in any of the equipment.

"Here she is," announced Bea, "Lucy Scott."

The man with no equipment turned. He stared at me for a second.

"Mrs. Scott?"

"Yes."

He recovered himself. "Forgive me. Speaking to that fellow downstairs, I assumed you were, uh, African-American."

"Here I am, just as I am."

He cleared his throat. "Mrs. Scott, we'd like to do a brief interview for Fox News Tonight. Is that okay with you?"

I mustered the strength to have no quaver in my voice. "Yes."

"Fine, fine. Now for our legal department."

He extracted clipboard and pen from a satchel, "if you'd just sign here and here."

He put the paper on the kitchen table and held it down with a finger. He handed the pen to me.

"What's this for?"

"Just releases us from liability, misstatements, blah, blah, blah."

I signed. He returned the document and pen to his satchel. He turned to the cameraman.

"George?"

"In a minute. Like to get a close-up of the family photo and the child's birthday note."

"Right." He turned to me. "My name is Rex, Mrs. Scott. I'll be doing the interview." He gestured in Bea's direction. "Your neighbor said you have a picture of your son. The one who died in Iraq."

I brought it up from my waist and set it on the table.

"Right." He looked at the man setting up lights. "Terry, need a position for her in which George can also get the photo in a pullaway while we're talking."

"No problem," Terry said.

"Joe, mike us."

Joe attached lavalier mikes to the top of my blouse and to Rex's lapel and returned to his post.

"Sound levels good?"

"Perfect. Controllable bounce. Love these high ceilings."

Rex rubbed his hands together. "Great."

He turned to me. "Now we sit. You, there," pointing to a chair, "and I'm across from you."

The cameraman said, "If the kid who did the lettering is around, be a good shot. Expand the story."

"Good idea, " agreed Rex. He looked at me.

"Is the child around?"

"I'll get him," volunteered Bea. She turned to her cell phone, punched in numbers. "Carlos, is Benjy down there?" Pause. "We need him at Lucy's." Pause. "Yes, he'll be on TV." She laughed. "Sure, sure, send Tony up as well."

She smiled at us. "Coming up." She turned away and punched another number. "Fred, Benjy and Tony are coming up. Don't call me and don't knock. I'll let them in when we're ready."

She turned back to Rex. "Okay."

He nodded. He looked directly at me. The cameraman was standing behind me to one side.

"The fellow behind you is going to take a shot of me asking you a question or two. Then I'll nod several times as though you are speaking. We'll pause and he shifts to my side. I'll start with the same questions and this time you answer me. Is that clear?"

"Yes." I said. "First you talk, not me."

"Okay. Video rolling?"

"Rolling."

"Sound."

"Sound on."

His demeanor changed. His eyes turned serious and he leaned slightly towards me.

"Mrs. Scott—may I call you Lucy?"

A pause as he peered at me intently.

"The demonstration in support of you is massive. Was it your idea?"

Another pause.

"That's good," said the cameraman. "Now give me a series of nods."

Rex nodded several times.

"Okay," murmured the cameraman.

"Now we shift," said Rex. "Terry, the photo of her Army son will be at an angle next to her."

"Got it." He moved the light around.

The cameraman moved around the table to stand beside the interviewer.

"Everybody ready?" Rex asked. Nods. He looked at me. "I'll ask the same questions to start. This time you answer."

I nodded.

"Video."

"Rolling."

"Sound."

"Clear as a bell."

Again his eyes turned serious.

"Mrs. Scott—may I call you Lucy?"

"Certainly."

"The demonstration in support of you is massive. Was it your idea?"

"No. My friends in the building came up with it."

"I understand you have a great many friends here at The Russell House."

"All ages. They're wonderful." Despite my resolve my eyes moistened. "My son cannot understand that I have a wonderful support group here. He's concerned for me and wants me to have good care. But I'm not an invalid!"

"I'm told you have friends of all ages here. In a moment I'll be talking to two of the younger ones.

"Right now I'm looking at a family photo of your middle child. Tell me about him."

I looked down at the photo. "That's Steve. He was career Army and loved it. This is a picture of him just after his promotion to Lieutenant Colonel. He was so proud."

"He died in Iraq?"

I couldn't stop the tears. I reached into my pocket and brought up a tissue.

"Excuse me."

"Take your time. The loss meant a great deal to you."

"Yes. My husband had passed away a few years before. And then Steve. He was in a convoy going to relieve . . . I forget the name of the place. It was before the Humvees got extra plating. One of those things by the side of the road exploded. Blew up his vehicle."

I dried my tears and regained my composure.

"Lucy, we reached your surviving son on his cell phone a few minutes ago. He told us the matter of moving you is a private family matter. Other than that, he had no comment. What do you say?"

I took a deep breath.

"I am very proud of my son Jim. He has always striven for excellence and I am glad that his hard work for his company has been rewarded. I had my 85th birthday last month. He is concerned that I am in declining health. But I am still able to get around. This is my home. This is where my friends and many social involvements are. I want to stay here."

I stopped and blew my nose. Rex looked at me and nodded.

"Okay. Cut."

He turned to Bea, who stood by the kitchen counter. "Are the kids here?"

"I'll go find out."

As she moved into the other room, he turned in his chair so he could see the cameraman.

"Did you get the wall photo and the birthday note?"

"Sure did. Got a steady twenty seconds on each."

"Good."

"Lucy, Lucy," came a shout from the living room. "The moving van's gone!"

Rex turned around as Benjy and Tony raced into the kitchen and stopped, suddenly all goggle-eyed and shy at the sight of the men and equipment.

"Hi, boys," Rex said. "We need your help. Will you help us?"

Wide-eyed, they both nodded.

"Let's start with your names."

"I'm Benjy and he's Tony. We're pals forever."

"And you live here?"

"Up on six," replied Tony. He added, "My dad's an officer on the Queen Mary!"

"That's great. I'm sure he's proud of you."

They stared at Rex.

"I have a nephew who's about your age. Let me guess. Seven?"

They nodded.

"Good. I need your help, Benjy and Tony. But let me introduce us all. I'm Rex."

He pointed at the others. "That's Terry. George and his video-cam. And Joe is the sound man. He makes sure everything sounds all right."

"Are we going to be on TV?" asked Benjy.

"If you help me, probably so."

Benjy and Tony gave each other a high-five.

"Now what I'm going to do," continued Rex, "is put a special microphone on each of you. And then we'll talk, okay?"

While the two were being miked by Joe, Rex gestured to Bea.

"Are their parents around?"

"In the hallway."

"Bring them in." He reached into his jacket pocket. "I need them to sign releases."

Bea left and returned in a few moments with Carlos and Angie.

"This is Benjy's father and Tony's mom."

"Hi. Glad to meet you both." He explained the paperwork that was needed and they both signed.

"Great. Now here's what we're going to do. Who made the birthday note that's on the wall?"

"Me," said Benjy.

"Okay. I want everybody to be really quiet while you tell us about making the note. Is that all right with you, Benjy?"

"I guess so."

"Call her Mrs. Scott," prompted Carlos. "It's more polite."

Benjy nodded.

"Now," Rex said, "everybody quiet. Benjy, I'm going to ask you why you made that birthday note and you tell me. Talk as long as you want. Okay?"

Benjy nodded. "I wanted to do something special—"

"No, no. Wait for the question. When I point at you, then you talk."

The kitchen was quiet.

"Sound."

"Sound rolling."

"Benjy, why did you make a very special birthday note for Mrs. Scott?"

He pointed his finger at Benjy and nodded. Benjy took a deep breath.

"Cause I wanted to do something extra special for her birthday. She knows French and Spanish and she's lived forever and ever and she helps Tony and me with problems."

He paused and looked at Rex.

"That's good" said Rex. "Cut." He turned to look at the cameraman. "Now I want the two of them with her."

"Got it."

He turned to the boys.

"Come over on each side of her. That's good. Now do something that shows you like her."

"Oh, my," I said.

The boys looked at each other. Each lifted an arm and placed it along my shoulders, overlapping.

"Good." Rex smiled. "Now, all three of you smile."

He grimaced. "Tony, a relaxed, natural smile, please. That's better. We're going to start the camera, and, Tony, when I point at you, I want you to tell me what is so special about Mrs. Scott."

The room fell silent. We three smiled. Rex pointed his finger at Tony.

"Mrs. Scott, she's the wonderfulest!"

He paused and was preparing to go on.

"Cut, cut, cut. That's good, Tony. Very sweet."

He looked at the three other men. "Are we covered?" They nodded.

"Thank all of you very much. We're done."

He stood.

"Will we be on TV?" asked Tony.

"I'm pretty sure. Good story. Fox local news at six."

The crew got their equipment together and left with good-byes all around. As they got on the elevator, I heard Tony proudly announce, "Tonight, six, Fox local news."

I rose from the table and went to the window. With the moving van gone, the crowd was beginning to dwindle.

"Bea," I said, "I'm going downstairs to thank everybody."

"I'll go with you."

Fred and the hallway guardians took the stairs. I thanked them in the lobby and then the lobby guardians. I walked outside. It was a lovely sunny afternoon. People cheered as I walked through the throng, thanking them.

When I went back upstairs, the *Daily News* was on the phone. I gave them a brief interview, repeating much of what I already had said.

At six all my close friends were with me crowded into my living room. We watched the news anchor highlight Veterans' Day activities around the city. He then turned to Rex, now wearing a natty sports coat.

"And it was a very special day for an eighty-five year-old widow in Brooklyn. Here's Rex Johnson to tell us more."

Rex turned to face the camera. "That's right, Tom. It was a very special day for Lucy Scott." Footage and commentary followed. My statement was included. Benjy and Tony were included. Not a dry eye in my living room when it finished.

There was silence as I pressed the 'off' button on my remote.

Finally Fred spoke. "You did it," he murmured.

"No, you all did it. I am so very, very grateful. How about a round of ice cream and cake?"

They cheered.

My telephone rang fifteen minutes later. It was my son.

"Hi. Mom." He paused and cleared his throat. "I've just come out of the Board Room. The Directors and I and other senior officers of the company were watching the interview."

"I hope your feelings aren't too hurt."

"Well, I've had better days but it's been okay." He paused again. "Mom, I really appreciate what you said. Being proud of me and affirming who I am. Thank you."

"I love you," I said quietly.

"I love you, too, Mom. First thing in the morning I'll call the place on Long Island and cancel the contract."

"Thank you."

"Talk to you soon, Mom. 'Bye for now."

"Good night."

I slept well. I begged off from a sleepover with Fred and went straight to bed by eight.

One last hoorah in the morning. The front page of the *Daily News* had a helicopter shot of the crowd in front of The Russell House below a headline that read:

Elderly Mom to Son:
Nix Stix, I Want to Live in Brooklyn!

19

It was early evening Thursday, three days after all the excitement. Everything was back to normal, or perhaps I should say, forward to the new normal.

We were just finishing the weekly food packs.

"I don't know about you guys," remarked Daisy, "but the last couple of days have been a real letdown after all the excitement on Monday."

"I know what you mean," replied Carlos as he stuffed a final oat snack in his sack. "Still looking for a job."

I looked around. "But you all were marvelous. Think of that amazing turnout!"

Mr. K smiled. "People from almost every apartment. Stunning!"

"Great interview on the news Monday afternoon," said Angie, smiling at Mr. K. She looked over to Tony and Benjy. "And you two were fabulous on the evening news."

Tony exclaimed, "We're famous at school!" He and Benjy did a high five.

I smiled at Bea.

"And you got the media involved."

"Glad I knew some people to call. Lucy, who was that woman hugging you in the hallway after your interview?"

"That was Pru, my daughter's friend. She told me Sophie backs me one hundred percent."

Fred grimaced. "It all was great, and Lucy's phone call from her son was icing on the cake. But here we are now and I agree with Daisy. How do we keep the energy flowing?"

Abe entered the conversation.

"What we are is a steering committee for next steps. I nominate Queen Bea for chair."

Rebecca waved her hands excitedly. "Yes!"

Bea smiled. "Thank you but no. I cast my vote for Fred."

We all turned to Fred and shouted, "Yes!"

Fred laughed. "I should have known that the proposer gets the job. Well, thank you, thank you. I accept. Okay, it's still the time and it's still the place. What can we do to keep the energy flowing?"

The kitchen was silent for a moment. At last Daisy spoke.

"Outside on Monday I talked to at least a dozen people who have trouble keeping their pills straight. Plus Lucy. Morning, noon, night — it gets confusing for us older folks. I volunteer to help folks to keep their pills straight. I'm an *expert* on pills!"

"And if they're willing to switch pharmacies, I can deliver," noted Mr. K.

"It all sounds good," said Fred. "Keep thinking about how we can help to build a sense of community like we had on Monday."

Abe nodded. "Here's something this episode has taught me." He looked at me. "Lucy, I keep thinking about how your son Jim completely misunderstood your situation here. I'd like to work with caretakers and family members of residents who live here. Help them to assess realistically what's needed."

Rosa chimed in. "I met mothers on Monday with children in their twenties who haven't found a good job yet. Yes, the economy still sucks, but I know some people at work who are good at resumes and finding contacts. I'll talk to them and see what we can get going with periodic meetings here."

"Hey let me be first on the list," said Carlos. "I've gotta find a job."

Bea looked at him. "I've been thinking about that. We have a problem here that may be a perfect opportunity for you. We all heard from Lucy's son a week ago that the management company has gone bust. I knew that was coming but didn't know the extent of the problem. Carlos, I've seen your resume. You have good people skills *and* a good handle on financial management. How would you like to be the Resident Manager in residence? We can work out terms. Are you interested?"

Rosa clapped her hands and Carlos exclaimed, "Absolutely!"

A broad grin from Fred. "This is great news. Bea, what about you? How else would you like to be involved?"

"I'll be busy making sure the demolition plan gets squashed. Then there's the issue of the dumpster, the exterminator, and the exterior brickwork that needs some repair."

"Need any legal help?" Abe volunteered. "I'll work with you on that."

Daisy spoke. "I think we need some social events for the whole building so we can all get to know our neighbors better. Let me think about theme nights and stuff like that."

Fred nodded. "Friends, these are all great ideas! Keep thinking. It occurs to me that instead of being a steering committee we could be the first installment of a Residents' Advisory Council."

"Great idea!" Mr. K agreed. "I'll be glad to help out with a monthly newsletter so everybody knows what's going on."

"Right," exclaimed Carlos, "and how about a Town Hall meeting periodically? A time to talk about issues and plans."

"Yes," said Angie. "With refreshments. I'll help with that."

"It all sounds good." Fred looked at me and smiled. "Lucy? Now?"

I cleared my throat.

"I have an announcement. Fred and I are engaged! We plan to marry early next year. All of you are invited."

There were excited murmurs and exclamations of congratulations around the table.

"And then?" nudged Fred.

"A honeymoon in Paris."

"Oh," breathed Daisy, "Paris at last! The Eiffel Tower! Montmarte! Shopping at Galeries Lafayette!"

"And," I broke in, "flowers for the grave of Edith Piaf!"

Daisy clasped her hands over her heart.

"Oh! Springtime in Paris! Just like the movies used to be! Is this a happy ending or what?"

Mr. K beamed at me. *"C'est magnifique!"*

www.ingramcontent.com/pod-product-compliance
Lightning Source LLC
Chambersburg PA
CBHW050411030726
47503CB00006B/2140